Probably THE World's Best Story about a dog AND THE girl who loved me

Also by D. James Smith
The Boys of San Joaquin
Fast Company

D. JAMES SMITH

Probably THE World's Best Story about a dog AND THE girl who loved me

A RICHARD JACKSON BOOK
Atheneum Books for Young Readers
NEW YORK   LONDON   TORONTO   SYDNEY

Atheneum Books for Young Readers
An imprint of Simon & Schuster Children's Publishing Division
1230 Avenue of the Americas, New York, New York 10020
This book is a work of fiction. Any references to historical
events, real people, or real locales are used fictitiously.
Other names, characters, places, and incidents are products of
the author's imagination, and any resemblance to actual events
or locales or persons, living or dead, is entirely coincidental.
Book design by Sonia Chaghatzbanian
The text for this book is set in Life.
Manufactured in the United States of America
First Edition
2 4 6 8 10 9 7 5 3 1
CIP data for this book is available from the Library of Congress.
ISBN-13: 978-1-4169-0542-4
ISBN-10: 1-4169-0542-1

For Dick Jackson

chapter ONE

The hands move to the sides in a series of small arcs: things being in order, a *plan*.

I'm knocking tennis balls across the almond orchard behind the house with a genuine Louisville Slugger that Uncle Charlie gave me. Rufus, my dog, is fetching them but not bringing them back; instead, he's carefully dropping them in the weeds like they were kittens he was going to come back to play with later.

"Georgie, get those balls, will ya?" I say. It is August, nineteen hundred and fifty-one, and it is hot. Georgie's my little brother. He's six—looks up to me.

"How come I got to get the balls?" he asks.

"'Cause Rufus ain't."

"How come you get to do all the hitting?"

"Because I'm on the baseball team and you're not."

"Why did Uncle Charlie only give you a bat?"

"Because only I need one." Georgie gives that a thought. He still hasn't moved a muscle in the direction of the balls. Rufus has come over and rolls on his back, looking and smelling like a bundle of wet straw, eyes peeking out, but, as usual, those eyes slipping off in two directions at once.

"Say, Paolo . . . ," Georgie starts. My name is Paolo—you say it "Pow-low," 'cause it's Italian. "Paolo," he says again, "how come Uncle Charlie is killing himself?"

I know better than to answer all his questions because he won't ever stop with them, but he's got me curious. "Well, who said that, Georgie?"

"Mom told Grandma, 'That man's been killing himself for years.'" Georgie looks at me with his big walnut eyes. "How come it takes so long to kill yourself?" Uncle Charlie has lived with us for as long as I can remember, lives in the attic of our old two-story house. I have six sisters and three brothers and a deaf cousin named Billy who lives with us too, and, still, our house is big enough we could take in Uncle Charlie and more if we had to. We'd make room if we didn't have it.

"Well . . . ," I say, "it's . . . kind of a big job."

"Uncle Charlie is a hard worker, isn't he?"

"Well, sure, Georgie, but now he's retired, he's taking it slow." Uncle Charlie used to work as a coal miner in West Virginia, but I've never seen him do a lick of work except to go down to the grocery to cash his government check and get a six-pack of Hamm's beer and a carton of Camels.

"Why he want to kill himself, anyway, Paolo?"

"Well . . . Say, you going to shag those balls or what?" I don't have any more to hit, and Rufus has got up and gone back to his "kittens" and is moving them off to another spot under an old mulberry tree.

"Why don't we go ask him?" Georgie says.

"First of all, 'cause he's asleep, and second, it ain't a polite thing to do, Georgie. You don't go asking grown folks about their work. It's like asking them how much money they make."

"You get money for killing yourself?"

"What?" I start off to get the balls before Rufus chews them to pieces.

Georgie suddenly finds his little-kid legs and scurries after me. "Paolo, you suppose we'll ever get jobs?"

"I'm twelve, and I've already had lots of jobs."

"What sort of jobs?" he asks, all suspicious. Georgie thinks I tell stories, which is not true, as it is well known that Ernie, my oldest brother, is the storyteller in our family. He's already twenty-one. I asked him once what was the difference between a lie and a story, and he said it's a story if they believe it. In that case, I would say that, mostly, I am not a liar.

"Shoot, Georgie, I've worked busing tables at the Downtown Café, was a private detective, a handyman, a roofer, and I told fortunes for a nickel each at the church picnic last summer. Remember when I told Mrs. Tuttle her dog was going to have six litters of pups in a row, that her sister in Iowa was going to marry an oilman from Arabia, that someone was going to steal all her prize oranges?"

"Nope."

"Well, can I help it if you got a memory like a six-year-old?"

"Did that stuff happen?"

"Just the last one, but . . . that's not the point." I stop dead in my tracks and swing round to look down at my brother. "Say, Georgie, how would you like to work for me?"

"Doing what?"

"Well, it just occurred to me, you're old enough to hire out to the neighbors to do yard work and such."

"I am?"

"Why, sure. Once when I wasn't that much older than you I painted Mr. Stevenson's entire fence."

"Really?"

"Well, of course." I don't say that I had to on account I had spray painted it with PAOLO, THE GREATEST IN THE WORLD, and when my dad saw that the red paint on my hands matched the sign, I had to, or else stay in my room for the summer and read the *Encyclopædia Britannica.* I'd already read it, so I did the fence job.

My dad isn't a mean one, so he doesn't smack me or anything—never would. He uses Chinese mind torture. I don't know where he learned it, as he came from the Appalachians, and they grow mostly yellow-haired kids with blue eyes like my dad and myself back there.

Well, the evening of the day I did my sign on Mr. Stevenson's fence, we're having dinner. Mom, who's Italian and will only speak English when she wants to, hollers us kids in to eat, hollers something incredible—as if we'd got lost or been stolen by

5

gypsies. My mom thinks there are gypsies everywhere just waiting to steal kids or, worse, put the evil eye on you. I've never actually seen a gypsy, but I know what the evil eye is. It's just like Chinese mind torture.

My sisters had made enough spaghetti to fill one of those little red wagons, and they'd dumped it on a big platter in the middle of the table, making a little mountain we were all working our way up, when my dad put the evil eye on me. Did it when he saw me reach out with one of my red hands for some meatballs. That eye, laid on my hand, put it to sleep like a dentist's novocaine. I pulled it back, slow, and let it drop, heavy, in my lap. Now, I knew my other hand had some red paint on it too, so I left it to rest with the other. You'd think somebody would've said something or noticed I was just sitting there, but of course my brothers Ernie and Hector were too busy winding spaghetti into their faces to care and my sisters were jabbering their sister stuff to one another.

At some point I decided to nab a slice of bread and started working my fingers across the table like Indians sneaking up on a wagonload of goodies when

I felt my whole self getting solid like a log that's been floated too long in water. I looked over slowly at my dad. He had one brow raised over that terrible eye, which—with a rod of righteousness shaking out of it and coming, probably, all the way from the Old Testament—was pointing right at myself, the very air shaky with its authority.

That's a torture I can't ever take, so I excused myself, and it was a relief when Hector came up to my room later and said, "Hey, squirt, Dad says you're to paint Mr. Stevenson's fence." Hector is eighteen and smart as a genuine professor; he's short, has shiny quick eyes like a field mouse, and hair that is one kinky wave, barber-clipped short to keep it out of trouble.

"I guess I should've cleaned up my hands," I said.

Hector, who was standing there with a book he's reading, looking over it and down his nose, said, "Maybe 'Paolo, the Greatest in the World' painted four feet high clued him in."

Hector loved my squirming at being ignorant, but he pretended otherwise, always acting as if he were just reporting what was obvious and didn't take any particular relish in having to inform me. I looked at the book he had. *Odyssey* it said on the spine. "That any good?" I asked, to change the subject.

"Well, yes, actually, it's quite good. It's a story of a journey—"

"Oh, a travel book," I interrupted.

"Well, not exactly." Hector was taking me seriously and was about to launch into one of his lectures, those kind that are more interesting to the one telling than the one listening, and I started practicing my looking right at a body whilst I'm in a trance, like Dr. Hypnotico at the county fair last year. "You see . . . ," Hector said. I had my eyes right on his mouth, but my mind was picturing water swirling down a black drain.

Georgie wakes me from my remembering when he asks, "How much you suppose I could make doing yard work for folks?" He's squinting past me, so I look too and see Rufus swallowing a tennis ball. Now, any other dog, that'd kill 'em. Not Rufus. He's as big as a Shetland pony and in his time has already eaten a beach towel, some firewood, three of my sisters' dolls, and the hat of our neighbors' Japanese gardener. That gardener was so mad, I thought he was going to give himself a heart attack. If you ask me, he had a temper problem. His face was leaking sweat like old plumbing near to exploding when he came to the door and asked if I was going to pay for the hat. I said I didn't speak Japanese. I motioned with my hands that he should maybe take care to get out of the sun and closed the door.

Later my dad got wind of all that and gave me three dollars that I had to give Mr. Harimoto to get himself a proper hat. Said from now on to keep Rufus off the neighbors' hats and clothes or anything else he might fancy munching.

"Well, Georgie, I suppose you could make twenty-five cents an hour, and let's see, after taxes and what I'd have to charge you to do your taxes and my management fees, why, you'd clear at least four cents. Shoot, why, maybe . . . even a nickel."

"Paolo, why do I need managing?"

"'Cause you'd be a professional, Georgie. All professionals have managers."

"How come you always got to boss me in everything I do?"

"When is it, exactly, that you do things, Georgie? I mean working things?"

Georgie sticks out his lower lip.

"Aw, you don't have to worry; I wouldn't be bossing you at all. You wouldn't even have a boss. You'd be working for yourself. I'm just offering to manage the business end of things so's you'll be free to concentrate on the working part. It's just how it's done, Georgie."

"What neighbors are going to hire me, you think?" he asks. Rufus is lying in the shade of his tree now, looking satisfied and full. Georgie sits down and starts petting him. Georgie is Italian-dark, like my mother, and gentle. Together, he and Rufus look what grown persons think is cute.

"Georgie . . . suppose that we first give you and Rufus a bath, and then you go up to people's doors and ask them if they have any chores for you. Say you need to make some money 'cause your dog is sick and needs an operation."

Georgie's eyes fill up with tears like spoons of some dark medicine. "Rufus is sick?"

"No, no, silly. Not yet."

That bad medicine spills off and rolls down his cheeks.

"I mean, no, Rufus ain't sick—and won't ever be."

"You said . . ." He starts sucking air like somebody who's got a chicken bone in their neck or the way Mr. Quigley did in the hallway at San Joaquin High School when he got told his boy, James, got shot down by a Russian MiG jet fighter in Korea. The way I heard it from Ernie was that James bailed out over the ocean at the last second and was rescued by two dolphins and a navy frogman. Came back to Orange Grove City, California, last year, a hero. Brought one of those dolphins too. Keeps it in the basement in a Doughboy pool. You can't see it or even talk about it, as the North Korean government never gave it a passport and James Quigley's no dummy, even if his dad is a teacher.

"Forget about that, Georgie. I'm just saying that if you were to take Rufus along, it might help you get hired." He's hugging Rufus tight now. Rufus just groans but is patient and lets him until he decides to return the favor and starts licking Georgie's head. Rufus could be a lion if he wasn't a dog. He's part St. Bernard and part English sheepdog, minus their smarts. I sit down. "You know, Georgie, have you ever wondered what Mrs. Pineroe has got in that old mansion of hers?"

Georgie stops his sniffling. His hair is dog-licked up like the wick of a candle, and his eyes are wide and suspicious. "No," he says, so quiet it's hardly a whisper, but he knows—he's already part of my plan.

The hands held flat and pointed inward at one another are flapped in front of your face to show there is *trouble*.

"I wish Billy was here," Georgie says.

"Well, he's not, and it's better this way, as you won't have to split your profit." Billy is my cousin who is deaf. He's nine and is Georgie's best friend, and mine, too, now that I think of it. He is visiting his mother in Tarzana now and is supposed to be back in a couple of days. She left him to live with us because her boyfriend and Billy don't get along. Billy and I are altar boys together at San Joaquin Cathedral. I do the talking, and Billy does the ringing of the bells and the pouring of the wine and the water parts during the service.

"Go on now, Georgie," I say, and give him a little push.

"You don't have to rush me," Georgie says.

Mrs. Pineroe is the great-great-granddaughter of a raisin-growing king. Actually, he was the first man who had the idea you could grow raisins in these parts. He hired Mexican and Portuguese and Chinese and all manner of men to dig ditches off the San Joaquin River and water some of the desert, and it turned out the dirt here was the best in the world. He planted some grapevines and got going on his raisin kingdom. He had artists draw posters of water flowing everywhere and little farms busting with fruit trees and vines and such. Put those posters up all over Europe and sold desert to French people and lots of others. Anyway, he got rich enough to build a genuine mansion.

"It won't open."

Georgie is pushing on the wrought-iron gate that's about two blocks of driveway and palm trees from the front porch of that place. I give it a push with my hand, then my shoulder. "Thought it was rusted, but it's locked."

Rufus sticks his head through the bars and tries wriggling in but can't.

"Georgie, you give it a try."

"I don't want to."

"Aw, it should be easy for you. You're as little as a kid can get."

"I'm as big as anybody else my size," he says.

"Well . . . sure you are." I don't want to discourage him. I take his shoulders and stand him sideways and work him into the fence a little. "See, like that, just push yourself on through." He does it and is halfway there when he takes a breath and his lungs filling up make him get stuck. That starts him to panicking, and now he's crying and shuffling goobers in and out his nose and coughing.

I look around but decide that it wouldn't be right to just leave him. Besides, with a little imagination, I should be able to think of a way to get him through those bars. "Georgie, calm down."

He stops his fussing and looks at me, his lower lip quivering. "I can't," he says softly.

"Well, you just did."

"Aaaaah!" He goes to blubbering again.

"Georgie, we are at the very best place possible for you to get a job," I say. "Mrs. Pineroe has more money than she knows what to do with. She'll probably give you a quarter for the sight of you. How often you think she sees a regular kid in the flesh?"

Georgie isn't encouraged.

"Quit your squirming and let me help you." I grab the top rail of that fence and sling myself over in one simple move and come up on Georgie on the other side. I grab hold of his arm and yank as hard as I can, and he pops through and we both sit down in a crumple.

Georgie is looking at me as if I'm Superman or something, and I guess I am kind of amazing. "Should I still unlock the gate from the inside now so you can come in?" he asks.

I look around at Georgie and myself and see that we are both inside the fence. "No," I say, quiet-like, and leave it at that.

Georgie has stood up and dusted himself off. "What about Rufus?"

"Oh . . . yeah, sure."

Georgie opens the gate from the inside, and Rufus comes bouncing in and runs right up the two blocks of driveway and onto Mrs. Pineroe's porch, almost catching her big calico cat, which scoots up a wooden pillar and hops into a potted plant that's hanging there. Georgie and I run up quick 'cause Rufus can't tell he's been outsmarted and is trying to jump up and get that big cat. The cat knows its business and is just lying there, swishing its tail and half swatting down with one paw, mewling a kind of cat ha-ha that sounds like a baby squealing its displeasure. 'Cept that cat is actually happy it's got a Rufus to tease.

Georgie tackles Rufus, and they go to wrestling round that porch whilst I take a gander at things. The porch is made out of slatted wood painted so many times it's slick, and there's windows big enough to drive a Buick through on each side of the front door. It's a double door with stained-glass peacocks for windows. I hear a thud, thud, thud and look over and see Rufus and Georgie rolling down the steps together.

"Georgie!" I hiss. "Knock it off and get yourself up here right now." He's gone and mussed himself after I spent half an hour washragging him fit for customers. He lets go of Rufus, who just lies down in disappointment, then rolls on his back for a nap. Rufus is his own kind of dog, and I'd have no other. He's my second-best friend, next to Billy. Georgie is not my friend on account of we have to be brothers and love each other no matter what, and we do.

Georgie comes up onto the porch and asks, "So what do I say?"

"Well, just say you're looking for chores. Say you are of a mind to help out old folks and will take care of any little things she might need done. Tell her you will take a donation for your pains, though."

"Donation for what?"

"For yourself, Georgie."

"How much of a donation should I take?"

"Say you usually get donations in the one-dollar range."

Georgie opens his eyes wide in astonishment.

"Just say it and take what she gives you—unless it's nothing, then do some crying or some such."

"What are you going to do?"

"I'm not going to even be here. I'll be over in that bush." I point to a big hay-fever-looking thing snowing blossoms. "And don't look over at me for any reason whatsoever."

Georgie sighs a big little-kid sigh and rings the doorbell before I know it. I have to jump off the porch in a flash. Rufus jumps up and comes over to me and starts barking at the bush. I whisper for him to hush, but he doesn't. It doesn't matter because Georgie rings that bell over and over for ten minutes, the whole time Rufus barking at me real slow, like one bark a minute, to let me know he still knows I'm in that bush.

"She's not home, I think," Georgie says to me in a kind of whisper-holler.

I come out of my bush. "Maybe she can't hear. She's got to be ninety years old." Ernie told me that when Mrs. Pineroe was young, she was supposed to have been the prettiest girl in Orange Grove City. That ain't saying much, as Orange Grove has only one park, one little stretch of downtown, ten churches, and twenty-nine liquor stores. And that's nowadays.

Ernie said that way back when, she was going to marry a lawyer from San Francisco, but he took a fancy to her little sister at the last minute and dumped Mrs. Pineroe. Her sister even got married in the dress Mrs. Pineroe had made especial for marrying. But that dress must have been cursed 'cause it was so tight that the bride fainted at the altar. They never did revive her. Died right there. Mrs. Pineroe keeps the dress in her attic in memory of her little sister and every holiday sits and looks on it and cries. You can hear that wailing if you come by the house late any night that's a holiday.

Fact is, if you was to even look on that dress, you would never, ever marry. Ernie says he'd give a hundred dollars to own that dress. Says he ain't the marrying kind and that would seal things up proper and forever. Anyway, we walk back down the driveway feeling discouragement all around.

When we get to the gate, there is Theresa Mueller, standing next to her bicycle. "Hi, Paolo. What are you doing in there?" Theresa has a crush on me, and I tell you it has been a burden to me for some time. She's a redheaded girl at my school—John Muir Junior High—who has blue-green eyes that make you tear up at the sight of them, the kind that look like they would hurt to own. She's got a little singsongy voice that rattles my tooth fillings every time I hear it, and I wouldn't be sad if I heard she moved to Kansas without telling anyone, but I say, polite as usual, "Hello, Theresa."

"I declare, Paolo, someone might take you for a burglar."

"Really?" I say, perking up at that thought.

Georgie opens the gate and we come out. Rufus

goes round behind Theresa and sniffs the rump of her dress. She always wears little sundresses instead of jeans like most sensible kids. "I'm working for donations," Georgie announces.

"You are?" Theresa says. "For church?"

"For little kids," he says.

"How sweet, Georgie." But she looks at me when she says the sweet part. Bats her invisible redhead eyelashes.

"It's the least we can do," I say.

Rufus comes round the front of her, having decided he likes her, and puts his head on her handlebars. She looks at him and pulls back some, as if he was a big, dirty dog, dumb enough to start slobbering on her, which he is.

I grab him by the collar 'cause he looks ready to munch her dress. Georgie says, "I haven't decided what to spend my donations on yet."

I give him a kick in the soft spot back of one of his calves, but Theresa isn't really paying him any mind anyway. She's looking past us, past the gate, past the palm trees with their fat pigeons sitting heavy as dark fruit high in the branches. I turn and look with her, up to the top windows of Mrs. Pineroe's mansion and then the very top attic window, which is open. And there is what looks like a boy dressed in a blue shirt and blue sport coat. He's kind of hovering behind what could be some thin gauze curtains. Then a puff of air riffles those curtains and they roll sideways out of view, inside the room, and then they ripple back, and the boy is not with them anymore.

Theresa and I look at each other, and we talk very fast to one another without speaking, doing one of those radio transmission things that you can only do with persons you know really well. Scares me Theresa can do it with me: *Did you see that, yes I did, wasn't that weird, it sure was, glad you saw it too, yeah, what do you think, what do you think, hey we are talking without speaking, that's right, Paolo, well don't get any ideas 'cause it don't mean there's anything between us, oh yes it means exactly that and you can't deny it.*

I guess this was the start of my women problems—and more.

chapter
THREE

Both hands push out as if pushing someone forward with *encouragement*.

Billy is doing what he does some nights. He doesn't think anyone sees him. He's back from visiting his mom. It was Sunday and not our turn to serve mass so all day we'd just run around, both of us glad he was back and doing nothing much other than watching Mr. Harimoto do bonsai on our neighbor Mrs. Haley's trees. Bonsai is when you take a little tree seedling and grow it up in a pot. Then you keep twisting on it, sort of like Mr. Mitchell at school twists Rodney Paul's ears. That and you clipper it back so it becomes this teeny tree that is really a full-grown one, except small enough so you can keep it in a pot. They do it a lot in Japan on account they don't have much space for trees and like to keep things in check. In Japan you could have the Sierra National Forest in your own bathroom.

We also rode our bikes down to Russ Mueller's gas station for two Nesbitt's lime sodas. Russ is Theresa's dad, but I definitely was not looking for her. We got the money for the sodas for showing my sister Shawna that Billy had taught me seven new words in hand language. She's thirteen, a little bossy as sisters go, but she makes a mint babysitting and was kind enough to teach Billy all he knows of signing. She pays us a little to keep up on our learning. I have to learn the signs, as Billy is my friend.

Signing is a wonder of its own. You can spell letters and whole words and even little sentences with signs. Say that you wanted to say, *You are a bother.* That's a handy one. Well, all you do is point at them that's your annoyance and then karate chop one hand in between the forefinger and thumb of the other hand. You could make a face too, if you wanted. Or maybe you want to say, *I'm sorry.* Just make a fist and circle it round your heart and look sorrowful.

Anyway, Billy's back and it's night now. *Night* is one of your arms in front of you like the horizon, and the other hand is the sun going down in front of it. *Now* is both hands falling down in front of your body, sort of showing it. Your body is the present tense, which makes perfect sense, as your body can't be anywhere right now but exactly where it is. I go around in my head in the past and the future all the time, though. But that's my mind inside my head doing this. It's never done me any good that I know of, but I enjoy it. You can go anywhere in your mind as long as you don't go crazy and end up like those gold miner hermits in the desert, eating dirt and having conversations with burros.

We are supposed to be sleeping. Georgie and Billy sleep in the same bed, heads in different directions, and I sleep three feet from them in my own bed. Some nights like tonight Billy gets up and goes to the dresser and sits down on the floor and pulls open the bottom drawer. He takes out a flashlight and turns it on, keeping his hand kind of covering it. Then he fishes out all these scraps of paper he's saved all his life. He tears them off of school assignments he gets back from teachers. It's just these bits of things they've written. *Not a bad job, Billy. With some work, you might improve. Keep trying.* Stuff like that.

He tears off just the parts he likes and saves them like money. Then he reads them any night he's not feeling encouraged. I know I shouldn't have read those bits, but I bet you couldn't have not read them either, so don't judge. I don't judge Billy about it. Those papers wouldn't be any treasure to me, but to Billy they are. I guess he doesn't have any encouragement of his own inside of himself and has to fill up every so often.

Anyway, he reads them for a bit, doing some sniffling, then puts them away and climbs back in bed. I'm guessing his visit with his mom didn't go all that well.

I lie there watching the moon sitting in the tree outside our window, quiet and lonely as it always is, by itself every night, sort of peeking its face into the room for a little company. I decide that someday I'm going to give Billy some genuine encouragement. I point to myself and nod. That's, *Yes, I am.* Then I fall to sleep thinking on how.

chapter FOUR

The tips of the forefinger and thumb of one hand close together like a bird's beak as it touches the upturned palm of the other hand; to repeat this motion, which means "print," indicates a *newspaper*.

Billy has Georgie on the handlebars of his Schwinn, and I'm coming along on a broken-down Columbia my brothers fished out of the dump for me once. Rufus is trotting along like he knows where we are going, which he does not; never does. Billy has an old fisherman's hat on to keep himself from sunburning red as grilled salmon, which he's prone to. He's got the kind of skin that is invisible—looks like that thin stuff tadpoles squirm out from when they're ready to be frogs. You can see all the veins running everywhere and stuff. He's a true Appalachian.

He's not the best-looking kid and tends to dress toward the sloppy. Once my dad drove by and saw us walking together and so called me into his room that night to tell a long story on the foolishness of hanging around with bad characters and such. I finally figured out what had got him to worrying and told him that it was just Billy with a hat on that he'd seen me with. He just turned red and said something like, oh, well, of course it was true that in the case of relatives and friends, you did have to lower your standards some. Then he waved me off, a little uncomfortable but satisfied that with his bit of knowledge, that I already knew, I'd be fine. My dad's smart. Just old.

Well, right then Billy and I are heading down to the *Grove County Guide* newspaper office. My dad doesn't take the paper. Says it's gossip passing for news and you can get it for free at the Downtown Café from the waitresses or at church come Sunday. Or Wednesday nights if you are a member of the Ladies Altar Society. Says that to my mom, who is one of those ladies herself. She never says anything to that but acts twitchy and proud as a cat that's been laughed at.

So if we really want to read the sports page, we got

to go down and get it in the alley out back of the newspaper place when they are loading their truck. Mr. Hartoonian drives that truck and will give us a free paper if he's in the mood. His moods are on account of his son, Mike, who ran off and hitchhiked to Alaska to homestead some snow. Mike hardly ever writes, but when he does, he writes good ones. Tells about his sled dogs and his cabin and trapping critters to sell. Mike says he shoots one moose a year and eats on it all winter. Says he can make moose enchiladas, moose pie, moose lasagna—just about anything you could imagine he can make out of the stuff. Says moose tastes kind of like wild hamburger, soaked as it is in pond water and lily pads, forest leaves and sky that nobody's ever owned.

We know all this 'cause Mr. Hartoonian makes it an occasion when he gets one of those letters and reads it to everyone all over town, though folks think his boy is a fool for missing out on Orange Grove all his life. Ernie says Mike ain't in Alaska at all; says he went to reform school for stealing parking meters downtown. Of course, he wasn't really stealing them. He just got drunk and ran over them with his pickup. After he'd snapped 'em all off, he thought to put them in the bed of his truck and take them over to stack 'em behind city hall. That's where they arrested him. Judge Kinney said it didn't matter about Mike's intention, just all the mess and expense he'd caused.

Later he graduated to regular prison for doing I don't know what, Ernie says, and Mr. Hartoonian writes the letters himself. I don't know if I believe any of that—I've never seen the postmark on those envelopes, though, whether they say Alaska or not.

We roll up on the loading dock about one o'clock just as they are stacking the bundles of papers out there. It's August and hot. In summer we are, all of us in Orange Grove, like hot sheet metal the sun hammers thin.

"Hey, Mr. Hartoonian!" I shout. Billy waves, stops his bike, and lets Georgie down. Georgie runs over to Mr. Hartoonian, who is sitting in his truck in the shade waiting on the papers and trying to breathe in that heat or get a quick nap. Billy and I go over there too and climb up on the running board with Georgie. We all got our heads stuck in at the window. We keep still since we know how to be polite. Mr. Hartoonian is sleeping.

Mr. Hartoonian is a bull walrus of a man. Got a

white handlebar mustache that grows out and winds back almost to his ears. He's a really heavy guy. You wouldn't want to walk through a hallway with him. If he tripped or swayed one way or another, you'd get smashed. When he walks, he takes a step and then his hips and his belly swing round to catch up on him. My mom told me he's not really fat, just big-boned like some of her Italian people. I'd have to say, then, he has very big bones—if he died and they put his skeleton in a museum, most kids I know would pay to see it.

Right now, though, we are watching him with the flesh still on him. We don't care about him being fat. That's no different than being short or wearing glasses or speaking two languages or whatnot. Makes you more of an interest than most.

"You think he's dreaming?" Georgie asks.

"Might be. His eyes are doing like a dog when it's dreaming."

"What's he dreaming?" Georgie asks, looking me straight in the eye. He really does think I know every-thing. I wonder if that could be more or less true. Who knows me better than Georgie, except Billy?

"Dreaming of Alaska, I'd say. Sees Mike taking a

bath in a washtub in the kitchen of his cabin. Mike's got an Eskimo lady boiling the water, and he's trying to decide if he should cut his hair now, as it's three feet long."

Mr. Hartoonian opens one eye and looks at me, then goes back to sleeping—like a whale might look at you before it rolls back over into the ocean.

Billy motions, *Shhh.*

"Shhh yourself," I say.

"I don't need shushing," Georgie says.

"Nobody said you did," I say.

"Boys!" Mr. Hartoonian booms. He sits up in his seat and pushes his little driver's cap back on his head. Actually, it's a normal-size hat but looks pint-size on him. We have our heads inside the cab now, waiting on what he has to say.

He blinks at us.

Georgie raises his eyebrows.

Then in a very calm voice, almost a whisper, Mr. Hartoonian asks, "I'm guessing you are after today's paper?"

Georgie and Billy and I all nod yes in answer and also at one another in astonishment.

He resituates himself, rolls his neck and his shoulders, his flabbiness rolling in little waves after. "You want the whole paper or just the sports section?"

"Just the sports, Mr. Hartoonian."

"Good. I can give you mine." He fishes round on the floorboard of the cab, gets the sports page, and hands it to me. We all fall off the truck as if shot. We sit on the running board and open it up. We give Georgie one page that has pictures. That's about all he cares to look at anyway. Billy and I are interested in Willy Mays, the rookie fielder who got called up by the New York Giants from their Minneapolis team in May. He'd batted .477 for Minneapolis. Now it's August, and it's already clear he is going to be something special in the majors. We check the box scores.

"Yeah," I say. "He hit a homer yesterday." Billy looks at me and smiles. Billy doesn't play baseball that much, but he's a big fan. Georgie is done with his part of the paper. He rolls it up and stuffs it into his back pocket. He doesn't think we know that he reads the pictures to Rufus when they are alone. Been doing it since he was three.

We hear some little snapping-turtle sounds and look up to see Mr. Hartoonian is crunching on a pickle. We climb back up to him. He gives us a frown. Takes the littlest bite, trying not to make any noise. Georgie sniffs at him like Rufus would. Mr. Hartoonian sighs and pulls a jar from under his seat and says, "Help yourself, boys."

We do, and all of us have a quick munching party. Even Mr. Hartoonian smiles and shakes his head and snaps his pickle down right along with us. "Mr. Hartoonian?" I say. "Do you know if Mrs. Pineroe takes the paper?"

"Boys, I just drop the papers at the liquor stores and the café and the newspaper stand downtown. You'd have to ask the delivery boys. I drop the papers to them, too, over behind Sheib's Auto Body. She probably does, though. Gosh knows, she can afford it."

"You ever been inside that place?"

"Her house?" he says.

"Yeah."

"Well, I have. When I was a kid, she used to have the school over on Halloween—right in the parlor— for treats and to listen to scary Edgar Allan Poe stories. She was an actress, you know."

"She was?" I say. "That after she got jilted?"

"What?" he says.

"She never did have any kids, did she?" I ask.

"You know, Paolo, I don't really know, but you could ask Mr. Gladstone, the editor. They got stories about that family in the *Guide* going back to Genesis. He could look up anything. Why don't you run along now and ask him?"

Mr. Gladstone has a reputation of being a grouch; can't stand people and can't stand the boys who make his deliveries. We are a little doubtful about asking him anything. Billy signs, *But he owns all the information in town.* On account that's the truth as we know it, we get off the truck again and head toward the *Grove County Guide* building across the alley before we remember our manners. Billy remembers. Stops us and motions us back. We go back to Mr. Hartoonian. "How's Mike doing?" I ask. It's always polite to inquire after folks' relatives, we know.

"He's fine, boys." Mr. Hartoonian sighs.

"You get any new letters?"

"No," he says, quiet and flat.

"If Mike marries that Eskimo gal, will she make those sled dogs move out of the cabin?" Georgie asks. He's looking down at Rufus, who has his tongue strung low and dripping in the heat.

"Boys." Mr. Hartoonian's pointing with a finger

the size of a cucumber. "Mr. Gladstone is in that office right over there, and I know he hasn't had a visitor all day. I'd hate to think I kept you out here with him needing company like yours."

We turn back around, satisfied we'd been our politest. We like Mr. Hartoonian and all, but for some reason, today he isn't *that* interesting.

Make like your hands are controlling the reins of
a horse carriage and you are managing.

"Haven't got time right now, guys," says Mr.
Gladstone. We're in his office, which is just this box in
the corner of his newspaper factory. Walls are half
glass—from the waist up. Reminds me of a hockey
rink's penalty box. Mr. Gladstone's secretary, Lily,
who has her own box too, just outside his, grabs us
and tells us we have to get out of his office and sit on
a wooden bench she has there for waiters. She apolo-
gizes to Mr. Gladstone for our getting past her.

We do what she says and watch through the
windows and her door, which is open, to all that
machinery making news. It's really one giant machine,
like an engine and a clock together. Has a fine smell of
oil and a thousand noises making maybe what could be

a mad mechanic's music—shuffles and clicks and thump-thump-thumps, even a few strangled coughs and pinched whistles. Somehow, it makes me think of my mind, how it's always churning, making the words I can think or say or write down as I will. But this is just a machine, and I know it is Mr. Gladstone and his newshounds who feed it the words.

Awesome as that contraption is, we get bored, and knowing that Lily has better things to do than wait on Mr. Gladstone to call her to have us come in, we go ourselves when she is turned round, nosed into one of her file cabinets.

Mr. Gladstone is on the phone whispering some kind of hushed shout, kind of the hissing that a badger will make if it's cornered and warning you it's going to chew your hands off at the wrists if you come any closer. He covers his mouth when he sees us, finishes his ss'ing and hangs up. He says, "Where's Lily?"

"She's outside. You want us to get her?"

He zings me a dark look. "Boys, what *do* you want?"

"We want to know if you have any pictures of Mrs. Pineroe's ghost," Georgie says.

Mr. Gladstone just opens his eyes wide and, if you

can imagine this, taps his forehead into the air, once, like he's making an invisible exclamation point with it.

"He's just a kid, Mr. Gladstone," I say. "We were just wondering if you have any old newspapers with stories about the Pineroes and their doings over the years."

Mr. Gladstone has black hair that grows only on the sides of his head and is slickered back with oil to match the shine he has on top. Has a nose that is a little lightbulb. Wears red suspenders and a loose white shirt, sleeves rolled up. He takes a big sniff with that nose. "You guys aren't bothering Mrs. Pineroe, are you?"

"No," I say.

Billy shakes his head.

Georgie says, "We're going to help her."

"Because, Lord knows, she doesn't deserve it," Mr. Gladstone continues. He is looking at Billy. "What's the matter with him?"

"He can't hear you. He's a lip-reader. Talks with his hands," I explain. But it occurs to me then that Billy talks to me mostly with his eyes. His eyes can say a hundred things without even signing. All round his eyes those tiny muscles like puppet strings under the skin can whip softly this way and that, and once you know him, they'll tell you what he's thinking.

"Oh," Mr. Gladstone says. "Sorry to hear it."

Just then Lily comes rushing in. "I'm so embarrassed, Mr. Gladstone. I—"

Mr. Gladstone waves her off and, for some reason, looks at Billy instead of me. "Send these boys out to Mr. Henderson in circulation. Tell him to look the two older ones over and see if they'd do for delivery boys."

"Oh, we're not looking for jobs, Mr. Gladstone. Except for my little brother here."

"Lily," says Mr. Gladstone, says it like a threat. She hustles us out of the office then, right quick.

Billy signs, *Thank you,* to Mr. Gladstone through the window. Mr. Gladstone smiles with his mouth turned down like he's mad, but his eyes are all twinkly. Billy's also.

Lily, who is almost as short as I am, is acting as if she has splinters in both cheeks of her rear and makes us march off after her through the plant like we were her own special prisoners. If she weren't a secretary, she'd have made a good nun. Sister Alphonsias Ruth Ann, who taught me my catechism, could give you a thrashing that hurt for two days just by squinting in your direction.

Turns out Mr. Henderson doesn't even work there in that building. All we get is a walk to the door and a slip of paper with an address on it and instructions to go see Mr. Henderson there by two o'clock.

We fetch our bikes. Rufus gets up, glad we are back, gives Georgie's arms a dog-licking bath—those kind that feel like sandpaper and give your whole self a chill 'cause a dog thinks you're a dog too. I tell Billy and Georgie that we better go home, that we'll have to get our information on Mrs. Pineroe ourselves, but Billy won't listen. *I'm going*, is all he will sign. And no matter how I try to explain that they will never hire Georgie, Billy's determined. So Georgie insists he's going too. In my opinion, I've put in a full day already as Georgie's manager, but I have no choice except to go along—so as to be sure no one cheats him.

chapter SIX

Two fingers make the victory sign, and the web between these fingers is placed over and against the forefinger of the other hand. That is *applying*.

"You're in luck, fellas," Mr. Henderson says. He's a tall, rumpled man with a baggy face, eyes gray and tired as boiled meat.

"We don't need luck—we work." That's Georgie talking. My Italian grandpa Leonardo says it all the time. Georgie doesn't know what it means.

Mr. Henderson looks at him and smiles up a little out of his weariness. "Well, what I meant to say is, I have one boy who left a week ago, so I'm hiring. One. Hiring one." He looks at us from behind the little metal desk he's sitting at in the corner of a little tin building where the papers get delivered to the newsboys.

"You're the only one old enough," he says, jutting his chin at me.

I already figured on this and have my speech ready. "Well, thanks anyway, but we join up together or we don't join."

Mr. Henderson snaps a half-cocked look of curiosity at me.

"It was nice to have met you," I say. I stick out my hand to shake.

He looks at it as if it's a tarantula, tips back in his chair, puts his hands together on his stomach, and starts twiddling his thumbs. "Look, Paul-O," he says, mispronouncing my name, saying it like "Jell-O," the way folks do when they read it as he has from where I wrote it on the little application me and Billy and Georgie filled out when we first got there. "Lily called me to say Mr. Gladstone said—personally, mind you—that I am to do some hiring in this case."

Billy nods, *Yes, yes.*

I don't know what it is with Billy and his madness to get what little is left of our summer ruined with being paperboys. I just want to get back over to Mrs. Pineroe's and find out what's what over there.

"Paolo's my manager," Georgie says to Mr.

Henderson. "I'm taking donations in the one-dollar range."

"That so?" Mr. Henderson says, his eyebrows scrunching up high like two caterpillars with cricks in their backs. Gives Rufus a look where he is sitting next to Georgie with his eyes crossed. Then Mr. Henderson glances at me. Frowns.

Mr. Henderson says, "Look, I have my best boy doing his route and also this one I'm offering you. I need to hire someone. Usually, I wouldn't bother with three boys doing the work of one. But . . . I suppose you, Paul-O, could sign the papers, and there'd be nothing all that wrong with your buddies helping out."

I look at Billy and his eyes say, *Darn it anyway, Paolo,* and they say also, very softly and a little embarrassed, *Please.* And I remember about my intention to give him encouragement, so right then and there, my summer is ruined.

Two fingers of one hand are a knife moving
across the palm of the other hand spreading
butter.

"Sure, it'll be fun," Butter says as he's folding
his papers and snapping rubber bands round their
waists.

Georgie says, "Really?"

"Yes sirree," Butter says, this time winking at
Georgie. All the paperboy guys are there now, and the
place is a tremendous commotion, laughing and
shoving like in P.E. class, except there's a seriousness,
too. Everybody is pointed toward getting their chore
done and out of there as soon as they can because
that is work, I suppose.

Butter Schwartz is a big, chubby kid of fourteen.
I don't know if he has any friends. If I had to guess,

I'd think probably not. Got a complexion that's some shade of goat cheese and two actual rolls of fat on the back of his neck. Wears a yellow-and-white-striped T-shirt. He's a bit of a legend 'cause his mother drinks a little more than the average lady who lives at home by herself with a husband who was a bus driver before he was dead. She can't control Butter; won't even try to make him take a bath anymore. It's because she feels guilty for poisoning Butter's dad. Sugared his cereal every morning for a year with a bit of rat poison until one day it finally slipped into his heart and clogged a little pipe with an elbow joint in there. He was at the intersection of Clinton and Blackstone at the time and ended up driving his bus through the plate-glass windows of Woolworth's department store. The whole building burned down. Took the fire department a day and a half to put it out. Called fire engines from Fowler and Selma and Madera cities to help.

Mrs. Schwartz got away with it since her brother is the district attorney and never investigated a thing. Ernie says that's just one more example of how getting married can go wrong. Billy says there is no truth to this rumor whatsoever. Says how come we never read anything about it in the papers? Or saw any smoke? Says, too, it's a mean-spirited story and we should find out about Butter for ourselves. Says it's wrong to jump to a bad conclusion about a person. I guess he knows about that, as folks sometimes think all manner of nonsense about him on account he is deaf. We don't have a choice, anyway, because Mr. Henderson has assigned Butter to train us for a week.

Butter is looking at Georgie with little black olive eyes when he tells him, "You go over there and snag an extra paper from that big stack, will ya?"

Georgie does it without any bother. He's too little for Mr. Henderson to see him do it 'cause that giant stack is over Georgie's head and it blocks Mr. Henderson's view of things. Georgie stands on his tiptoes, and his fingers curl over the top of the stack and slip one newspaper off pretty as you please. He brings it back and hands it to Butter.

"Georgie doesn't do any stealing unless I tell him," I say to Butter. I already know they count out exactly how many papers they give you and you are not supposed to take any extras to sell on the street after you do your deliveries.

Butter turns. He's a foot and a half taller than me and outweighs me by sixty pounds, I'd bet. But I'm getting shaky with fury at his boldness. "You ever give Georgie an order again and I'll take a baseball bat to you. I don't care. I swear it." Georgie is my little brother, and if you have one, you know what I mean; and if you don't feel about it this way, you should and that's that. Okay, the baseball bat would be going too far, but you get the idea.

Butter's eyes are trying to drive two-penny nails into mine, but he knows I'm serious, and those eyes of his aren't hard enough, aren't nails or even marbles, just squishy little olives, and right then I know Butter would be a mean one if he could, but he can't on account he's got fear in him. I know that don't mean he's not a danger. Fear can make a guy do more to you than he would if he was just mad at you. Right then and forever after, I know I will have to watch Butter.

But for now he breaks out in a hearty smile. Punches out, soft, with a slow-motion jab to one of my shoulders. "Hey, I never had a little brother. I was jealous, I guess. Wanted to try it out. Okay?"

I don't even smile.

He turns back around to his paper-folding. "Check out how you do this, Paolo," he says over his shoulder. We are more curious than we are anything, so we all crowd round him where he stands at a long counter with little wooden partitions, one for each kid. He can fold a paper in one second, slipping it off the shelf above the counter, snapping a rubber band around it, and stacking it on top of those already folded. He shows us all that and then how to load the canvas bags we put the papers in. Hardest part is getting the bags on your shoulder—the way a cowboy in a movie carries his saddlebags—and then letting them slip off and onto the rack on the back of your bike all in one motion. Those bags are heavy, and I see right there one of the reasons you got to be twelve to do it.

Butter makes me do it five times 'cause I'm short and I have a bad time of it, trying to shrug that heaviness *up* onto the bike rack whereas most could let it slide off their shoulders and drop *down*. I can't tell if Butter is making me do all the practice to shame me, as there are lots of guys round there, or if he's just helping me get it right. One guy starts snickering until Rodney Paul, who is more or less a friend of mine at

John Muir Junior High and who is also an altar boy, tells him to shut up. I never knew Rodney had a paper route. I give him a secret half nod, but he goes back to his work without knowing me, as do the others. I guess I'm not officially one of them yet. Finally, I get how to do it, though it's not easy at all. It makes me feel kind of manly. There might be something to this work thing after all.

Both hands make fists. One fist taps the back
of the other fist three times, and in this way
you show **work**.

Next day we have our second training session with
Butter. It's Tuesday, and we are going to practice the
neighborhoods of his route and then do some collecting
of customers' money. Monday through Saturday,
papers get delivered around three in the afternoon, so if
we want practice time, Butter wants us early. That's
okay with us since come every Sunday, the papers will
always go out in the morning, and we have to get used
to that, too. Today we have to go practice throwing
some old papers and scout our route before we get the
real papers and do the real delivering.

So it's early. As usual, my dad isn't home. He's a
fireman for Southern Pacific Railroad and is gone three

or four days at a stretch. My mom and her dad, my grandpa Leonardo, ride herd on us most of the time. He's already at our house at six a.m., before anyone is even up, sitting at the kitchen table sipping coffee and reading yesterday's paper. When Billy and Georgie and I come in, eyes clogged with sleep, he looks up and smiles, his eyeteeth glinting. Grandpa is dark as a pecan, sort of round and hard and smooth as one, too. He can speak Italian and his own brand of English.

He's the most amazing grandpa you could have. Has his own little market and butcher counter, plays the saxophone, grows peppers and tomatoes and figs in his backyard, and has both his eyeteeth fitted out, really snappy, in gold. If you get anywhere in the vicinity of himself, he'll snatch you and hug you like a boxer will do when he's winded and won't let the other guy loose. Even though Grandpa is no taller than a kid, he can squeeze you good—until you're both staggering around the room. You'd think it'd hurt, if you didn't know it was love. He says we are his finest treasures in this world. So usually we let him near us, but this morning we are so sleepy, I know we are all keeping our distance, not wanting Italian-style hugging just yet.

"Yous boys get up for yous hungry?" He looks at us suspiciously. Grandpa is always suspicious that a person is hungry on account he came to America hiding in the bottom of a ship; came all that way by himself when he was eleven just so's to get three proper meals each and every day, the way we do in America.

Billy pours himself a cup of coffee. I'm a blind man trying to blink sight into himself. Georgie says, "I think so." Well, that's all Grandpa needs to hear, and pretty soon we are all sitting at the table eating sausage, eggs, pancakes, milk, coffee, orange juice, and a half grapefruit each. Grandpa watches us, measuring out with his eyes each bite we take and nodding with satisfaction at every swallow just as if it were his swallow and him enjoying the taste of it.

"Yous want some navy beans?" he asks. Grandpa will give you a bowl of steaming white beans any hour of the day, if you'll let him. He thinks navy beans will solve any problems you could get 'cause that's what he ate all the time when he shined shoes on the streets of Philadelphia. He could buy a bowl of navy beans at a lunch counter for five cents, and he remembers how that was a miracle to him when he was a kid. He's a little disappointed we won't have any, though we usually will eat them for him, except this time we just don't have the room. If our stomachs were the holds of ships, we'd have already sunk.

He lets us go to get dressed with our shoes and everything and on with our day once he's squeezed us each proper, his eyes closed and soulful. And we go slamming out the back door to get our bicycles and head off toward Butter's house, Rufus trotting along by our side and dog-smiling. He's our treasure, happy and willing the way that he is. It's seven thirty in the morning, and already you can feel underneath that cool a dead dryness that is the beginning of the day's heat to come.

We ride up the driveway of Butter's house. It's a white-wood, peeling-paint place with sagging steps up to the porch. There's a brown four-door Ford in the driveway, with grass growing up as high as the tires. The roof of the house is green, tan, and gray because it's been patched over with different shingles. There's a blue and red plastic parrot on a little swing that's hanging over the porch, and Butter's mom has bedsheets for curtains. We all nod and smile to one another, liking Butter's place a whole lot.

We ring the bell and wait. Ring some more. Wait. Nothing. Billy shrugs his shoulders and frowns.

Georgie says, "You think Butter accidentally ate some of his mom's special cereal?"

Right then a voice comes out the window so close to us that we jump back. "Goooooooood morning, campers!" The door explodes open and Butter comes out. He shakes each of our hands like he's the president of the United States and us his admirers. He takes us round back, where there's rusted car parts and rotted lawn furniture and where the weeds and grass are waist-high. There is a smashed-flat path to his bike, which he gets and wheels back to us. Rufus is in heaven, jumping around through all that mess, stopping and sniffing hard at the interesting spots.

We go out front and mount up, following Butter, feeling good to be riding in a group, just like a motorcycle club. Butter is showing us what will be our route. Route number 408 is four blocks by two blocks and in between our house and Butter's—about seventeen blocks from the *Grove County Guide*'s little tin building. Butter has his canvas bags and a few of last week's papers in them. He rides up and down one block showing us how to reach back, just so, and snatch one of those papers and then fling it onto a porch in one smooth motion.

Georgie and Rufus get themselves set down on the park strip of lawn to be our audience, their heads going back and forth following the action. You got to use your arm for power at the beginning of your throw and then your wrist has to snap when you let fly in order to get the paper to land exactly where you want it. You have to balance yourself and the bicycle all the while and keep it going in a straight line. It's one of those things that looks easy enough but isn't. Have you ever noticed that people think whatever you know how to do is easy and what they know how to do is hard?

Butter has Billy and me going up and down that one block practicing for two hours, until Mrs. Jennifer Wilcox comes out and asks us to stop. She is a young one and has dark hair and dark eyes and wears a silky pajama overcoat thing. Butter goes up on the porch and we follow. She slips back, half behind her front door, and thanks Butter for stopping. Butter is hungry to look at her housecoat because you can almost see through it. Mrs. Wilcox lets him, smiles, and says in a low voice, "Bye-bye," and shuts the door.

Butter drifts down the steps. When his mind comes back to us, he tells how she is lonely because her husband is in jail for rolling back the odometers on cars. She saves up money to buy cartons of cigarettes for him and to pay for a mail-order course he is taking in jail so he can be a minister when he gets out. It's all a con for the parole board. The two of them will go to Las Vegas to work the blackjack tables.

I look at Butter whilst he's doing his telling. "Butter," I say, "do you know my brother Ernie?"

"Your brother who works digging trenches for Pacific Gas and Electric?"

"Yeah."

"Nope, but I plan on working for PG&E myself someday. Wouldn't mind meeting him," Butter says. "Why do you ask?"

"I don't know." But I do know. What I didn't know until right exactly now is that there are persons who can explain things as well as Ernie does, and Butter is possibly one of them.

Butter is talking to Billy. "You know, you threw those papers as good as me. That's something, because I've been doing it for two years."

Billy is beaming, blushing, looking down at his

brown shoes, swinging one leg and scuffing an imaginary line in the sidewalk. He's forgot his hat, and I can tell he is blushing on top of the sunburning that's going on.

"When do we get the money from people?" Georgie says, standing, brushing lawn bits from his butt, Rufus getting up, too, stretching. They'd stayed put, watching us the whole time.

"Well, we can do some of that right now. It's almost ten and people will be up," Butter says, patting Georgie on the back.

We have to go to Butter's route, number 407, to do the collecting, as they are his real customers. The guy who quit our route already did his collections before he left. Part of Butter's own route is a section of apartments, the kind that look like the motels on the highway. They have a little grass area that the apartments are built around in the shape of a horseshoe, and each apartment looks like its own little house with a miniature porch and all.

We go round to them, ringing the bell, most of the people not home. We find out you have to wait after you ring the bell because old ones take an age to come to the door. You know they are still alive in there because they all have little dogs and those dogs wouldn't be doing any barking if they'd had nothing to eat and starved. They go half mad 'cause it takes their masters so long, shuffling to the door, I suppose. Butter gives the old ones big phony smiles and sirs and ma'ams them so as to get a tip. Their hands are shaky and soft in yours when they give you the money. I know 'cause Butter let me do the collecting at one of those apartments.

One place has a guy in his fifties with a crew cut and muscles still on him. He'd been a sergeant in Europe. Drove a tank through downtown Berlin right up to Hitler's basement. Used his .45 Colt semi-automatic to hold back a squad of Russians so's an American could be the first to come knocking. Butter says not to ask him about it 'cause he's pathologically shy and wouldn't admit it anyway.

Whilst we are doing the collecting, I notice that the names on the mailboxes don't match the names in Butter's collection book. His book has names like Harry Truman and Joe Louis and Jack London—names with that sort of fancy—but the names on the mailboxes or under the doorbells are all Jackson and Johnson and Anderson and the like. I ask about it when I see that Butter uses the ordinary names when he writes the receipts.

Butter explains that he isn't cheating the *Guide*. It is just that the company makes newsboys go out asking folks to sign up to take the paper. Says the company doesn't pay you for doing it, but you have to have two new sign-ups every month. Says it's an injustice the *Guide* gets away with 'cause we are kids. He's righting things by stopping the paper of one of his own customers and swiping an extra paper to give them for a few days until he can sign them up as a new order with a different name. He gets his two new sign-ups a month this way, but it makes his book-keeping a horror. Butter has some kind of backward thinking that goes something like this: It's so obvious the fancy names are probably fakes that Mr. Henderson would never suspect him of being so dumb as to use them and so thinks they are real. That must be the case or else Henderson hasn't the time to notice little stuff like that 'cause Butter's never been caught.

Billy listens hard to all this with his eyes, his mouth sagging open with wonder, and I see right off that work isn't a game, not even for kids. Butter explains that most kids do a paper route for about six months 'cause their parents think it will teach them something about life. Yet those parents make their kids quit once they find out it is exactly like life. Butter says that it isn't just having to get new customers without getting paid for your trouble that isn't fair, but also that if a customer moves and doesn't pay you, you have to pay the *Guide* out of your earnings.

He says parents also find out pretty quick that they have to help out days it rains or times their boy is sick and such. Butter has had his route for two years 'cause he has need of it. Just like a grown-up.

We finish with the collecting, me watching everything close. I know why Mr. Henderson assigned us to Butter. I don't think he knows about Butter's bookkeeping, but he knows Butter gets the job done.

We are looking up to Butter now and know we should buy him a Coke when we are through but don't have any money, so it is him that takes us over to Russ Mueller's gas station for a soda. Billy sits close next to Butter on the curb, and Georgie lies on his back with his head on Rufus, who usually falls asleep the second he isn't moving. We still got to go along with Butter to deliver the real papers this afternoon. I'm glad that we won't start our own route until the weekend because there is no way we are ready.

chapter NINE

One forefinger taps the side of the head to indicate the *mind.*

It's nine o'clock in the nighttime, and Margarita, my older sister, comes up into the little hallway at the top of the stairs going to our attic. There's a quiet spot there just outside the door to Uncle Charlie's room where I go to do my reading. I'm reading *Alice in Wonderland* by the light of a lamp that swan-necks out from the wall. The *Wonderland* book is a crazy, upside-down thing that gives me what Grandpa calls "mindkerflooey." He's been getting it ever since he came to America. Means things don't make sense and yet, at the same time, maybe they do. Means your mind gets stretched out like those fun-house mirrors. You can feel, well . . . like bubbles are floating up through your body to come snapping on the surface of a little dark pool in the middle of your brain. Some kind of crazy like that. Some little chills tickling up your back and then slipping down again. Some mindkerflooey is scary and bad, and some . . . it's the most fun you could have, the very best that good is made of.

For example, Mr. Gladstone, who's supposed to hate kids, came by the other day to ask Mom if he could take Billy to lunch. Billy told me afterward that Mr. Gladstone is friends with Mr. Weinchek, who owns the Downtown Café. Billy had a malt, a burger, onion rings, a side of coleslaw, and three bags of chips while those two spent the whole lunch sitting across from him in a booth drinking coffee and telling him all this stuff that added up to the notion that Billy could be anything he wanted, even a test pilot. Billy didn't tell them he was afraid of those kinds of heights and would rather be a cook on a submarine. He said the malt was the best part and also how they let him fill all his pockets with sugar packets before leaving.

"Paolo, you have a phone call," Margarita says. She's a quiet sister with dark, serious eyes who plans to grow up to be an Italian beauty. Sometimes she's my favorite because she doesn't want to know what I'm up to. She thinks boys my age are some kind of creature a good number of years away from being human. She isn't a snob about it, just figures there's no point in knowing my affairs. I think she probably looks at me the way I do a tree rat running along the power lines in the evening. I watch it and figure it knows what business it's about, but I've no interest in chumming round with it or knowing exactly what that business is. Like now she isn't asking me who it is calling. I know it is Butter. Wants to tell me to meet him for more paperboy lessons tomorrow.

I go down the little stairway to the second story and then down the big stairway that cuts one way then back again, down to the entry, where the telephone is. Our house was owned by rich people before it got broke in and homey enough for us. I pick up the phone.

"Paolo?" Theresa whispers, her voice kind of throaty and hoarse.

The hair on my neck stands porcupine tight. "Yeah?" I say.

"Meet me at Mrs. Pineroe's in fifteen minutes." Husky-voiced, excited.

"What for?" I whisper back, though I don't know why I'm whispering 'cause no one is listening to me and I'm not up to anything that's a secret.

"Fifteen minutes," she says.

She knows I'm interested in Mrs. Pineroe, but I know Theresa. "Look, Theresa." I sigh. "I'm not allowed to have a girlfriend until I'm old enough to get married." Now, that's only true on my Italian side. Grandpa saw my grandma just once at a dance where he was in the orchestra playing saxophone, and he sent a message to Grandma's dad and was married two weeks later. Turned out they didn't even speak the same kind of Italian, so when they get excited and fight, they don't know what they are saying—never end up hurting the other's feelings and are fond of each other to this day.

"Paolo," Theresa says, still whispering, "I'm thinking hard about something right now. Close your eyes and concentrate, and I'll bet you know what it is."

Against my better judgment, I do it. And I see the top story of Mrs. Pineroe's house with the sky running dark overhead and one of the shutters banging softly in the wind.

"You see it, don't you?" she says.

I blow air, loud, through my nostrils. "Give me twenty minutes."

"Sure, Paolo." Says *Paolo* with sweet hot chocolate drizzled on both syllables before the line clicks dead.

I go get Billy for protection—from her. Georgie is asleep, lying there with his feet pointed east. Ever since he found out the world turns, he lies that way so that when the world goes down to make the sun come up, he will be sort of standing and facing the sun in the morning instead of upside down like he'd be if he slept with his feet pointing west. It's a Georgie kind of mindkerflooey, but it makes me think he might grow up to be very smart or else seriously stupid.

Billy and I have to climb through our opened window because we aren't allowed out after nine. There's an overhang on the back of our house to shade what used to be the back patio, before tree roots made it into a jumble of bricks. We climb right out onto it and scoot along to where the fence meets the side of the house. We hang by our hands from the overhang till our feet feel the top of the fence, and then we let go and kind of teeter there for a second and then jump down, landing hard, knees bouncing when they take the shock.

Rufus comes up to us in the dark, wet-nosing my hand. We leave him in the backyard, as he might make too much noise. Not that we can make him stay without tying him, which we don't like to do. But I say anyway, "Stay." I know that means absolutely nothing to a dog such as Rufus. Probably on account Georgie isn't with us, though, he stays.

Our house is on the last block before you are in the country and the grapevines and the fig orchards and the orange orchards and such, so it isn't that far to Mrs. Pineroe's. We just follow twelve blocks of country down Pineroe Boulevard and we're there. We run all the way, forgetting our bikes in our rush. The moon's a big glowing zeppelin floating over the fields, following us and lighting our way. If it weren't there, there would be no way to see anything in the country at night. The figs look like dark bats hanging in the trees. We slow as we come up on the place that looks like a cluster of those monument rocks in the desert.

Theresa is nowhere we know. We hang around, sort of crouching near some bushes outside of the gate. Billy motions, *Let's go.*

I nod and start to walk quickly back the way we came, but he grabs hold of my shirt and motions, *No, let's go in.*

I don't see the point of that if Theresa isn't here to show us what she wanted to show us, so I shake my head.

Billy raises his eyebrows and smiles faintly. *Scared?*

So we hop the fence and slip up the long walk, me trailing. A dog's bark echoes lonesome in the distance—some farmhouse dog, I guess, longing for company or a rabbit to bother.

Suddenly, there is an icy hand on the back of my neck, and I go cold as a statue. Billy senses I'm not following him anymore and turns around. When he smiles, I decide it's time to breathe again, and Theresa slides round in front of me. "You came, Paolo."

"Yeah, I did," I whisper, a little hot with anger because even if I'm not fond of her, I don't like being scared in front of a girl. "Now, suppose you tell me why?"

"You don't know what day this is, do you?"

"It's Friday, August tenth."

"That's Mrs. Pineroe's wedding day."

"How would you know?"

"My grandmother told me."

"Really. No fooling?"

Billy comes up close to us to try to read our lips in that light.

Theresa faces him because she is polite and says crisp, to make sure Billy gets it: "I thought we might come and see if she goes up to the attic and cries . . . and, maybe, if she . . ."

"Meets anyone up there?"

"Yes, something like that," she says. She drops those watery eyes of hers. "You don't think it's wrong of me do you, Paolo? Are we Peeping Toms?"

"Shoot no. You have to be eighteen to be a Peeping Tom. We are just kids who don't know what we're doing."

She looks at me kind of funny.

"C'mon," I say to her and to Billy, and I take the lead going up close to the house, showing I have courage enough I could pass it out on Halloween if asked to.

That mansion looks like an old wooden church, except instead of a steeple, it has two sort of towery things sticking up on each of its sides, like rooks of a chess set.

We listen hard as we can but hear only the rustling of the eucalyptus trees the wind is bothering a little and that dog still barking somewhere off in the fields. "Could you climb up there and look in the window?" Theresa says, a snake's whisper, close in my ear.

I look at her. "I could, but why would I want to?"

"How will we ever know what it was we saw?" She looks genuinely disappointed. "Paolo, everyone always says we never have any fun in Orange Grove because it is too small. Yet right now we have a genuine point of interest, and you are letting it slip away from us."

Nobody talks like Theresa except herself. "Nothing slipping anywhere," I say. "And for your information, I have fun in Orange Grove all the time."

"If you are frightened, I'll have Billy give me a leg up and try myself." Suddenly, she's snippy as an older sister. No more hot chocolate dripped on her words. Already to the rat poison stage.

I grab her by the elbow as she starts off, and she swings round quickly and sags into my chest and looks up at me, soulful. I feel like we were dancing and she passed out. I push her back, arm's length, and prop her up on her own legs. "Just stay put."

I motion to Billy, *Let's give it a try.* He's all for it.

The only way up looks to be a redwood growing right next to the house. Has branches that come right down to the ground like a fancy dress that spreads out around a woman's ankles. We worm our way in next to the trunk and start laddering up. My hands get all sticky with sap and roughed up with scratches. Billy's, too. I know, 'cause he is grunting below me and sucking on the palms of his hands each time he gets up and snugged into another branch. We stick our heads out of the tent of those branches when we get to the top of the second floor.

There is a ridge about six inches thick that runs round the entire house like a line of icing on a big cake. I step out and onto it, back to the wall and looking down. Theresa is a face the size of an orange looking up at us, moonlight making it into a little paper lantern.

Billy's legs aren't as long as mine, and he doesn't seem able to make the long step from the tree to the ledge. He looks at me, eyes saying, *I want to, just can't.* I believe him 'cause I see how it's true.

I take a big breath and start inching my way along the ledge to a spot below one of the attic windows.

I'm looking for a way to pull myself up without becoming a bird with no wings. I know if I fall, I'll arrow straight down. All you'd find is my feet sticking out of the lawn like some of that modern sculpture I saw once in *Life* magazine.

Then a light goes on in the window of the third story, just above the ledge where I am. Below me Theresa disappears—her bright face hidden, quick, wavy, sort of liquid as if the night were spilling ink over it. I guess she's slipped into a bush down there. Billy has gone back into the tent of the tree. It's just me, plastered backward to the top of the house. I hear the window slide up, the old wood complaining.

I don't see anyone stick their head out or anything, but a sweet odor drifts up to me. Perfume? Ghost juice? And that's it. I'm stuck there, and the light of that window is a sharp thought awake in the mind of that house. Then it goes out. I get back into the tree, fast as I can, and Billy and I sling ourselves down. Theresa says she couldn't tell if it was Mrs. Pineroe or the boy we'd seen that day. Says it was just light seeping out into the night like honey and that's all.

We decide to get out of there. Helping Theresa

73

back over the fence, I am a gentleman and don't look where I shouldn't. Billy does, but he's nine and his look is the same he'd give a pencil or some tennis shoes, so it doesn't matter. I realize we could have opened the gate for her from the inside if we'd been thinking. We are going back up the road, a silent herd of clouds drifting slowly over us and the night air cool and a little wet. About a football field's distance from the mansion I stop, hold Theresa by the elbow, and say out loud and irritated in a way I don't understand, "If you are going to be going round with boys such as Billy and me, you better get yourself a pair of Levi's."

And instead of getting mad, she drops her eyes the way she does and looks back at me quickly, those river eyes of hers glistening. And she smiles shyly. I realize Theresa is a puzzle I don't want to try to figure out.

"Oh, forget about that," I say, suddenly hot. "I don't see any reason you need to be hanging round us anymore, anyway."

For a half second Theresa looks like I slapped her, and then, quick, she just frowns, a little sad, a little scared. "You don't mean that, Paolo."

"I mean it!" I hiss, but her eyes make me have to look away. And the breath gets punched out of me right then 'cause I see the light of Mrs. Pineroe's attic window in the distance is on again. And just as I look, it goes black.

chapter
TEN

The two fingers of the victory sign snatch an invisible something from under the forearm, the V sliding up from elbow to hand. The snatching of the fingers is to *steal*.

Uncle Charlie has only two pictures on the wall of his bedroom. One is Jesus, who looks more Appalachian than Italian—he looks Italian in the paintings at San Joaquin Cathedral—and the other is a photograph of John L. Lewis, the big boss of the United Mine Workers, a kind of saint if you're mountain Baptist. Not a real saint like Saint Lucy of Sicily, who my mom has a statue of she keeps on the mantel of the fireplace in our living room. Saint Lucy can see everything from up there and keep a watch on us all. Ernie says when he was little, Mom used to carry Saint Lucy around to look out all the windows when it was storming to keep the sky from lashing our house with its lightning. Says Mom gets Saint Lucy to do all kind of favors for her by praying to her in Italian. Has to do that in a whisper for it to work.

He told me, once, when Mom asked Saint Lucy to look out for him and Hector to not ever get in trouble anymore with the teachers at school, that Saint Lucy wouldn't do it. Mom got mad and put masking tape over Saint Lucy's eyes. Said, "If-a you don wanna look out-a for these-a boys, then-a you can no look at nothing." When she's mad or by herself, she always talks my grandpa's brand of English or else just straight Italian. But she cooled off in a couple of weeks, after Ernie and Hector took care to stay out of trouble. She's a generous one. Took that tape off. Said, "That's-a better. It's a-nice a-this way, eh? You can-a see now everythin-a you want."

Anyhow, I know Uncle Charlie won't know nothing about the Pineroes since he was a West Virginian all his life, but he is also the smartest person I know, and we're both usually glad of each other's company, play chess and checkers sometimes, so I'm up outside his room the very next day after we went out to the mansion.

It's a Saturday. Uncle Charlie is sleeping in. Billy and I getting home late last night made me not wake up till just now myself. And thinking about Theresa. How she split off from me and Billy walking home with that hurt-girl face. It's already eleven o'clock. I wait on Uncle Charlie until I get tired and then slip into his room. I'm not in there, now, to wake him, as that's rude, but maybe just to move around a little till he decides to hear me and wake up. But no matter how hard I try to not wake him with my shuffling and coughing and bumping into things, he stays put under his blanket. Finally, I go to shake his shoulder, and there's nothing there but pillows and blankets. I should have known. Uncle Charlie is only five foot six inches and bone-knob skinny. His bed is usually a mess and looks pretty much the same with him in it or out of it. It's just that he's mostly in it.

There's only one other place to look, and that's the front porch. I jump downstairs and fly out there. Uncle Charlie has a big upholstered chair that he sits in to play checkers and smoke and sip Hamm's. He's sitting there, head back, so still, he could pass for dead if he cared to. In fact, I pull out a pocket mirror I have and hold it over his mouth to see if it fogs up.

He snaps both his eyes open and snatches me by the wrist. Eyes drilling holes in the air above him.

"It's just me, Paolo," I say, quick, 'cause Uncle Charlie is one of those lean little fellows who have muscles that are thin but strong as bridge cables and my wrist is smarting awful. His blue eyes are soft as creek water, whites of them chock-full of veins like tiny strings of trout's blood trailing off in that creek. They slide over me, and his grip lets up. He breathes as if the sound of it hurts his ears, and he closes his eyes, taking care so they aren't a bother to him either.

Ernie says if you drink Hamm's beer all night that the whole day after your body burns from the inside with invisible flames and your brain is a dried corncob with the corn nibbled off, then tossed on a pile of garbage to go soft in the sun, horseflies swarming over it. So I never drink. That and I feel mostly happy without it. But I never had no Irish girl when I was a coal miner in Virginia that ran off with Horace Riley, the clerk in the ladies' half of the shoe store. Never found that out whilst I was a mile under the ground, stretched on my stomach, scratching coal so's to have enough money to marry that girl who was promised to me by her own self.

I'm looking at Uncle Charlie and wondering about what Georgie said—all that about my uncle killing himself. I watch him for a bit, and I don't think his keeping his eyes closed is to fool me into thinking he's asleep so I'll go on and leave him be. I sit down on a wooden stool that's out there for those that feel like getting themselves whipped at checkers. I lean in close and start soft. "Uncle Charlie? Uncle Charlie, I know a guy who has this girl always trailing him." I watch him for a reaction.

Nothing.

"Well, the guy is too young for marryin' and so is the girl—least ways, in California she is." I'm looking at his thin arms, a scratched gold wristwatch with a worn leather band around his wrist. Then I notice his left leg twitches once on its own. And his eyes stay closed, but his mouth moves.

"I'm bettin', sometimes, you like that girl hangin' round," he says, voice scratchy.

"You really think so?" I say, quick, so he won't go back to sleep.

"I do," he grunts; opens his eyes and rolls his head sideways to look at me and still keep himself comfortable. "You take her along sometimes when you're going places, don't you?"

"Well . . ."

"She talks, you talk back."

"Yeah, but . . ."

"She calls you on the phone, and you run and answer."

"I never ran."

He smiles. His teeth are getting brown from tobacco.

"Honest, Uncle Charlie, the last thing I told her was to stop hanging around me."

"Okay," he says. "But you asked, Paolo, and I'm telling you it's natural for a fellow to be curious about a girl. Natural to find her tiresome, too. Both those naturals are on account you ain't a girl yourself." He smiles again, this time it's more of a smirk.

"But . . . Uncle Charlie," I say, "I think she's liable to kiss me without being invited, and . . . on account Mom made us into Catholics, I could end up married. Heck, by the time I graduate high school, I could have four kids and still be driving a bicycle." It's all tumbling out in a rush.

"Paolo," he says when I take a breath.

"I might . . ."

"Hold up a second."

". . . be the youngest—"

"Stop!"

That surprises me and I quit. I hang my head, a little shamed he thinks he needs to be hushing me like some kid.

"Now," he says, gentle as a man with a scared dog he's fond of, "ain't none of that goin' to happen to a boy that doesn't do anything."

The sound of his voice makes the air go out of me like a tire tube softening down.

"Ain't nobody can make you do a thing you don't already want to do yourself, Paolo."

"Even a girl?"

"Not even a *girl*." Says *girl* like he's saying *crocodile*. I smile.

He smiles back, just a little smile this time, more a tremble of one side of his mouth, all that talking having worn him out. Closes his eyes, rolls his head back, nose pointing at the roof of the porch.

"Uncle Charlie . . . ," I whisper.

He exhales as if dying and goes completely and immediately asleep. The screen door squeaks. It opens a crack, and Maria-Teresina-the-Little-Rose, my four-year-old sister, peeks her face out. "Paolo," she says. She doesn't say anything else, though I wait on her.

She's got appley cheeks and curly hair that looks like a couple of hundred blond question marks Scotch taped to her head. She is the last of the litter and got her Italian name because my mom got to name her. Dad said he would've called her Helen Louise O'Neil. Right now I can't tell if she's just wandered out here or forgot what it is she got sent to tell me.

"You can come out," I say.

She shoots a look at our uncle and his big chair, then round the porch with its one little stool and the stack of newspapers with a checkerboard on it. "Shawna says, 'Paolo should come in here and get his mail.'" Says it exactly as Shawna would, words clipped short with a pair of sharp scissors.

I don't know exactly what that could mean. I never get any mail except from Maxus Inc. I sent them a post-card once when I saw their ad in the back of a comic book, so they keep sending me stuff about the Amazing Spy Kit. I don't see what the rush is for Shawna since I've never had the two dollars, ninety-five to order it and won't this time either. But I say, smiling at Maria-Teresina-the-Little-Rose, "Okay. Thanks, sweet pea."

"I'm not peas," she says. Sticks out her tongue and leaves. I hear her hard little shoes inside on the wooden floors as she walks away: THUMP, Thump, thump, thump.

When I go in, no one is in the entry to our house at the bottom of the stairs where the telephone is and the little table on which the mail is always set. I open the envelope that has no stamp and no return address. Read what's written in the middle of one whole page of yellow paper in little looping letters:

If you want Rufus back. start saving your money.

And that—*that*—is mindkerflooey as bad as it gets.

chapter ELEVEN

Take your index finger and make a scratching motion close to the side of your forehead and that means **suspicion**.

My mind is latched on the lead-glass window of our front door, watching a thistle of sun trapped in the lines of the lead and the glass; but my stomach . . . it's a fish slapped hard onto land, trying to flip itself over. The phone rings. I flinch. I pick up but don't speak.

"Paolo, is that you?"

I know it's me 'cause I'm breathing.

"It is, I can tell. You know, you are old enough to say hello, Paolo, even if you don't feel like talking," Theresa says.

"Hello," comes my voice from a long way off.

"Is something the matter, Paolo?" she says, no longer miffed, only concerned.

"You could come over if you want," I say without thinking, and hang up. I definitely do have mindker-flooey 'cause I'm thinking about Georgie and grammar. I'm thinking a noun is a person, place, thing, or idea. An adjective describes a noun. Georgie knows Rufus isn't a *human* being. But to him, I know, it's the noun, the *being*, that counts. And he's probably right. Rufus is a being that isn't human, but that's all. He's a whole being. Has feelings like any human.

Georgie's sitting on the floor with Maria-Teresina-the-Little-Rose playing Scrabble, though I don't know what rules they have. Neither of them can spell, but they're both studying their chips and moving them around. I'm not looking forward to telling Georgie what's happened, so I slip by and go out back myself and look around, even though I know Rufus won't be there.

I sit under the oak tree we have growing behind the garage of our house. It's where Rufus sleeps in a bear hole he dug for himself. 'Cept he sleeps in it in summer to stay cool instead of the winter like a bear would. He sleeps in the garage in winter. We tried him sleeping in our room in the house, but every single time he heard a cat or something, he'd start that slow steady barking of his. After you woke up and hushed him, he'd wait one minute and then bark one more bark. You'd hush him once more, and he'd bark once more. He thought it was a conversation.

I don't know how or if I should tell Georgie anything about Rufus. (Rufus = noun: *being;* adjective: *special.*) I glance up and see Billy walking, casual, across the yard toward me. With Theresa. Coming over, she must have latched onto him.

I don't beat around the bush. I just show them the dognapping note. Billy starts walking in circles and starting off one way and then halting, then starting off another way, until Theresa grabs him. Looks him in the eyes. His eyes are doing that same rushing round his feet have been doing. Theresa just looks at him steady until he slows down inside. She can do Dr. Hypnotico better than me. She nods slowly to Billy and leads him over to me. She sits down, and Billy does likewise.

We talk the whole thing out. Takes us I don't know how long. We go over it fast and then slow and fast again. One, we figure out that there is no reason to put up flyers about a lost dog or to check the pound because Rufus isn't lost. Two, there is absolutely no one we can think who would steal Rufus. Three, the only thing we can know is that it's money we need, and we don't even know how much or how long we have to get it. Four, we have to tell Georgie because he will miss Rufus, for sure. If we say Rufus is lost, Georgie will go looking day and night, and that'll take all our time—trying to keep track of him or else end up with a lost Georgie.

And, in fact, right now Georgie is coming down the back steps of the house. He's got Maria-Teresina-the-Little-Rose with him. She's the only one he's old enough to boss, though even she isn't one easy to manage.

"Yes, you have to," Georgie is saying to her. Georgie has Rufus's leash in one hand and Maria-Teresina-the-Little-Rose in the other hand, and he is starting to lead her across the yard. "Rufus is hungry, so we got to feed him, and I'll show you how," Georgie is saying.

At the sight of them we all hush and stand up and go still. I look at Theresa, and her eyes are little rain puddles when she looks into my eyes, which are probably red with worry.

Will you tell him, yes of course, I really would appreciate it, I know, I'm asking for Georgie's sake not mine, I'll do it for both *your sakes.*

"You are a stinker, Georgie," Maria-Teresina-the-Little-Rose is saying in the sweetest voice you can imagine. She's not insulting him, just saying sentences she knows and likes the ring of.

"I'm not, and you are my sister and not allowed to say so if I was," Georgie says.

"Hey, Georgie!" Theresa calls out.

The two of them look up and cock their heads sideways, wondering what Theresa is doing there in their backyard yelling to them. Then Billy waves them over, and they come running, having a tough time of it 'cause they are holding hands. They have enough trouble at their age coordinating their own running, much less the both of theirs together.

Georgie looks at each of our faces and frowns. He thinks he's going to have to be part of another plan of some sort. Maria-Teresina-the-Little-Rose is looking at Theresa's dress. A girl is a girl even at four years old, and what they think is of interest will forever be stupid stuff: doodads and ribbons and hairstyles and beads and the like. The way they act every time they spot one another, you'd think they were Plains Indians on a trading mission.

But to her credit, Theresa gets to it right off. She kneels quickly, her dress flaring out like a parachute to close softly around her. "Georgie," she says, "Rufus has been stolen by someone awful, and we have to get some money to buy him back. Now, don't you get too upset because we *can* get the money and we *will*. And we'll buy him back *right away*."

Georgie looks at Theresa.

"Do you understand, pumpkin?" Theresa asks.

One eye of his squints at the pumpkin part. She isn't one of his sisters, and he knows he doesn't have to listen to what she says. So he looks at Billy. Billy nods. He looks at me. I nod. He swings back to Theresa.

Maria-Teresina-the-Little-Rose says, "Rufus is hungry."

A hundred little tadpoles of tears swim up into Georgie's eyes. He's thinking a whole lot of things, you can tell by his face, and we wait on what he will say. But, finally, he says only this: "That ghost did it." Says it sure. Says it bitter, and a little afraid, too.

I look at Billy and then Theresa. Billy's face is a blank, but Theresa's eyes are narrowed and thinking. I'm wondering why we don't all have mindkerflooey. I think it's because, somehow, what he's said doesn't exactly sound that crazy.

chapter TWELVE

"Nope."

"Yep."

"Nope."

"Uh-huh."

"Uh-uh."

"Yes."

"No."

"Stop." Theresa puts a gentle, cool hand on my arm. She thinks Georgie and I have sufficiently discussed the matter of his going with us or not. Or so she says—something like that. She goes on to say, "He can't do much harm, and he might actually be of some help." She lets her eyelashes swat the air in front of her slowly in a way she probably thinks is fetching.

"He has to be round here for my sisters and mother to watch. If they knew Rufus has been dognapped, they wouldn't let Georgie out of their sight for two seconds," I say.

"Well, for now they don't know."

She has a point there.

But then she asks, "Will your parents be mad if we take him without asking?"

"They'll be a lot madder if he runs off after us by himself, and he *will* follow us," I say, chewing my lip.

Billy has his long-billed fishing cap on backward, the way he does when he's mad or means business, and he couldn't care less, I can see, about Georgie tagging along or not.

Maria-Teresina-the-Little-Rose is running toward the house as if her little, fat-bottomed red pants are on fire, even though she doesn't understand what's going on at all. "Okay, we better go now," I say. We'd already wasted a few hours just sitting out there talking and pondering. To have your dog stolen and getting a note about it is troubling to a person more than you might think. Theresa is the only one of us that seems to be enjoying us all sitting there together. I'm sure she's worried about Rufus too. It's just that she's such a girl, she can't keep her mind off of me. Sits close and touches my hand now and then when I talk about what if Rufus gets away from who it is that took him. Or how he could go wilding—running through fields and maybe get stuck in somebody's barbed-wire fence or get hungry and eat up something he shouldn't. Lots of farmers leave all kinds of poisons out for coyotes and varmints.

But he might not. Theresa says that Rufus ain't people smart but he's pretty good at being a dog and can take care of himself. I don't know about that. Billy signs that Rufus takes off on his own lots of times and comes home when he's done sniffing and visiting. But I can tell by Billy's eyes he is worried, keen as can be. I tell myself maybe Rufus is just lying around eating food and lapping up water wherever it is that he's locked up.

I know my folks might help us out if we asked, but I think they would be more in the way than not. They are the type that grew up in the country, where animals are not people and that's the way of things, and would only mostly care that we learned that instead of we find Rufus. I know all about that since I grew up in what is mostly country too, and sometimes I think about animals like they do. It's just that I've known Rufus since we both were little, and that makes for a fondness that is the way of things too.

But it's now going on six o'clock in the evening, and it's a Saturday also, and that means Grandpa and Grandma will be coming to dinner and my dad will be home any minute. We just cannot wait around anymore, even if we don't know for sure what we're doing.

We take our bikes. Georgie on Billy's handlebars and Theresa on mine, as she didn't bring hers. "Theresa," I say, my breath heavy with pedaling, "you know no ghost stole Rufus, right?" Actually, I'm still not totally sure, but I don't want to look foolish.

"Right, no ghost."

"So what are we doing?"

"We both understand that the Pineroe mansion is the only thing we know of that doesn't add up."

"Yeah, that's sort of my way of figuring too, I guess." And I do think she's more or less figured it right.

"And, Paolo?"

"Yeah?"

"Do you remember that the entire time we were out there that night, a dog was barking off somewhere close by?"

"Well"—I stop pedaling for a second, and we almost go toppling over before I start up again—"yeah, I do remember. But there's dogs barking in the country—and the city, for that matter—all the time, day or night."

"Yes, I know, but there was something about that particular barking that bothered me at the time. I just didn't think too much about it because we were so busy."

"Yeah, but we left Rufus home that night."

"You left him home. The question is, did he stay home?"

I don't see how it would be possible for Rufus to get stolen and brought to the mansion before Billy and me got there. But he could have run to Mrs. Pineroe's by himself. I doubt it, though, 'cause why wouldn't he have found us? Heck, the whole thing is hard to figure. It could be he was out there sniffing round when we were busy with our spying and someone or something out there really did grab him.

Theresa has an imagination that seems set on scaring me sometimes, and I do not know why that is. Maybe she's one of those persons that is so smart, they get confused and ignorant about regular stuff. It doesn't matter; I got to do everything possible to find Rufus, and if Theresa is willing to help, I'm willing to have her around.

We come up on the gates to the mansion and stop. Even in plain daylight, the big house looks impressive and unhappy in some way. I don't waste any time in jumping the fence and opening up for everybody. We go straight up the long winding drive. As we come up to the porch, Georgie says, "I'll just ask for my donation, and you guys can run in the door when she answers."

Everybody stops. We are surprised that he can do that much thinking of his own. Billy's face is curious. Theresa says, "Well, why not? Let's have him do it."

"I don't see the point."

"She's more likely to answer the door if she sees just one little boy. I know that's the way my grandmother is."

Theresa has a grandma whose mind is like an old lantern with the works inside nibbled down by some moths so that almost no light shows anymore. Just a sputter flaring up now and again when she'll remember Theresa's name or something. Theresa takes care of her so she can still live in her own house. I suppose most kids would do anything for their grandparents, but still, to my mind, it is a genuine credit to Theresa.

We all tiptoe up onto the porch and crouch to the side of the double doors of wood and stained glass. That glass is five or six colors of a peacock tail fanned out because there are real peacocks that live round that mansion and always have, Hector has told me. A peacock makes a calling noise that fades off, sounds like the world going dark, if dark had a sound—a long, heart-tight, sorrowful sound, like sadness for the day having to end. Georgie rings the bell, and just then we hear it: a peacock calling. Calls once and then again, then hushes.

And the door opens slowly. A white-haired lady with a crinkled brown bag of a face leans out. She stoops over to see Georgie, her whole body a question mark. When she sees him properly, she straightens up, but her back doesn't straighten up all the way, as she's old.

Georgie is staring at her, not making a peep. She's got a light blue dress on that looks like it's made out of a thousand lace doilies, and it goes from the tips of her toes right up to the top of her neck. She blinks slow at Georgie, her eyes two glassy black stones, the kind that old arrowheads are made of. She smiles, seems a little confused for a second, but surprises us when she says, "Would you and your friends care to come in?"

Nobody moves, though Georgie looks over at me.

"Now, now, you've been here before and inspected my house, even the roof, so I think we should meet, don't you?" She turns away from the door and starts off for one of those rooms they call a parlor.

Theresa, who has gone pale, shrugs her shoulders and turns her palms up. Georgie and Billy are already following Mrs. Pineroe inside, so we go too. But I whisper to Theresa, "Watch yourself." She nods yes, and for the first time, I see fear in her, and it is a satisfaction of some kind to me.

"Sit, sit." Mrs. Pineroe motions to us. "I'll be back in a moment."

We all take a seat on these red velvet chairs,

except for me. I make the mistake of sitting on a little couch, and Theresa slips in next to me. But I don't care 'cause we're looking round at Mrs. Pineroe's gear. She has pictures hanging on the walls from wires—horses with fat bellies and stick-thin legs galloping, all four hooves off the ground; one of a man with a Moses beard and the big button eyes of a raccoon; one of two girls with a cocker spaniel at their feet looking up at them, the dog and the girls with the same kind of haircut and curls. There are lamps with glass earrings hanging off of their glass shades and pillows with tassels spread all about.

But what has Billy fascinated is this stereoscope. I know that's what it's called 'cause Theresa tells us, herself getting prissy with the telling and losing her fear. It's a binoculars contraption that you can look through and see two pictures exactly the same that come together to look like one picture of something. Makes it like you could walk into that picture, if you cared to. Billy and I are shuffling through all the pictures there on a table, loading up one of women standing on a beach with some kind of swimming dresses on, when Mrs. Pineroe sticks her head out of the swinging door to the kitchen.

"Miss? May I have your assistance, please?"
Theresa is the miss, and she jumps up and goes in
there in a flash without even looking at us or saying
anything. She's right back out in a minute with a tray
of iced lemonade that we set to slurping in a hurry.
Mrs. Pineroe drifts back in and sits down in a chair
next to Theresa and me. Theresa is the only one of us
not drinking her lemonade.

Georgie wipes his mouth with the back of his
hand and is just about to speak when he slams his
eyes shut with a wince.

"Ice-cream headache?" I ask, and glad of it, too,
as it might keep him from blurting out something we
don't want blurted.

He nods.

"You have a beautiful place here, Mrs. Pineroe,"
I say.

"Thank you. My name is Alexis Pineroe, and
yours is . . . ?"

I blush, though I don't know why, except Mrs.
Alexis Pineroe has a way of making you feel like a goof,
maybe because she's as sweet and polite as can be.
"I'm Paolo O'Neil. This is my little brother, Georgie,"
I say, pointing him out where he's now on his knees

on the floor holding his forehead. "That's Billy, my cousin." Billy is helping Georgie back to his chair.

Mrs. Pineroe looks at Billy with her eyebrows crinkled. "Child?" she says to Georgie. "Child, are you all right?"

Georgie nods, and you can tell he is fine 'cause he's enjoying Billy's attention. Billy gets Georgie situated and then looks over at me and Theresa.

Theresa clears her throat.

I look at her.

She makes a little cough and then puts the heel of her shoe over the big toe of my tennis shoe and smashes it until my eyes start to tear. Mrs. Pineroe is still looking at Georgie and doesn't see that. I guess I'm supposed to introduce Theresa like she's a relation or something.

"And your name, dear?" says Mrs. Pineroe, turning to Theresa.

My toe tells me I should speak up, and I say, "This is my . . . this is Theresa Mueller."

"Oh, you are William's girl," Mrs. Pineroe says right off.

"William was my grandpa. He's passed on, ma'am. My father is Russ Mueller."

"Oh, I am sorry, dear. William was a sweet boy. Played the piano quite well. Did you know that?"

"No, ma'am." I think Theresa is surprised by what she is hearing.

"Played a duet with him right on that piano there on a Christmas Eve when it was so foggy that the boys had to sleep in the barn and go home after breakfast."

Theresa's mouth is dropping slowly open.

"Do you play, dear?"

"N-no."

"Oh, well, all young ladies have to play. You come by any afternoon you like, and I will teach you. It will give you something to keep your beaus calm. And they do need calming, I'm sure you know." She reaches over and pats my hand, so I must be a beau, whatever that is, and I admit, right now, I do not feel calm.

"Do you know you have a ghost that's a thief?" Georgie says. He's stepped right up to her because she isn't scary to him anymore. He's not even angry. He just wants to know.

Mrs. Pineroe puts her hand to her mouth and looks at him, blinks twice, and is thinking hard, you can tell. Finally, she says, "No."

Billy gets Georgie by the shoulders and pulls him away from her face. Theresa stands up suddenly, spilling her glass of lemonade. I can't think of a thing to say.

Billy signs to me, *Get a towel.*

Mrs. Pineroe watches him sign, her eyes soft as a deer's.

I stumble quick into the kitchen, where I look round for a dishrag or something. I find one over the sink. It's hanging on the faucet, which is really a small pump handle. I come back and try to blot up the lemonade that has put a dark spot in the round carpet between the chairs and the couch.

Theresa takes the towel from me.

"Do you know someone lives in your upstairs where you keep the wedding dress your sister wore when you got jilted?"

Mrs. Pineroe looks at Georgie. Looks at Theresa and Billy. Looks at me. For the first time since we've been there, she doesn't seem strong. Seems shaky. If Rufus weren't Rufus, I'd wish we hadn't come, hadn't made her eyes swell up wet when she says, "It's true, at present, I'm not living alone."

chapter THIRTEEN

Take your fist with the thumb sticking out and stroke the side of your chin, pointing out the strings of an old-fashioned bonnet = *girl*.

Take both hands with the index fingers pointing up like a cowboy with two six-guns and swing them, one, then the other, at yourself and then out front of yourself = *talk*.

All the little dots of twilight are flying in and roosting first in the trees and then tiptoeing around on the lawns, gathering together, and then the darkness settles in. We are sitting on a bench on Mrs. Pineroe's porch. She's asked to speak to Theresa alone. First, she asks her stuff like does she know what she's doing running around with boys in the evening. I know 'cause I have my ear and my eye to one window that isn't quite closed. Then, she tells how she knows how interesting boys are, that she was married when she was sixteen to a producer who took her out singing on the stage, which is not the life you would imagine. Mostly sitting in hotel rooms and eating bad food and making your parents ashamed for breaking your original engagement to a proper attorney. Says she ended up in Havana, Cuba, singing in a nightclub. Her husband got sick and was dying, and it was awful when he stopped yelling at her the way he did when he was well. Says, "Imagine that? All that time, him being a beast of a man, and then he gets too weak to be beastly and you are sad."

She rattles on with that sort of stuff until she says, "Promise me, Theresa, that you will not be too quick to marry."

"No, ma'am," Theresa answers.

I think Mrs. Pineroe is a good influence for Theresa.

"Ma'am?" Theresa asks.

"Yes, dear."

"Is the boy upstairs your son . . . I mean, your grandson?"

"I have no children," Mrs. Pineroe says, and stiffens in her chair. I can see her perfectly there in a little pool of lamplight. I can't see Theresa. Nobody says anything for a bit, and then Theresa shows she's a clever one and a hard one, too.

"We've seen him, Mrs. Pineroe," she says.

At that Mrs. Pineroe shows herself too. "Do you know that I am personal friends with the police chief, the district attorney, and the editor of the newspaper?"

But Theresa shoots right back with all this pleasantness squeezed in tight in her voice, "I understand that, Mrs. Pineroe, but those boys out there, they only understand what they want, and then they just go after it without thinking."

Now, this must have impressed Mrs. Pineroe because she reaches over and takes Theresa's hand and pulls it into the light with her. "Men are like that, aren't they? It's we that have to watch over *them*." She pauses, then takes a chain she has around her neck, and I squint hard through the crack in the window shade where I'm watching to see what is on that chain. "Henry is my sister's grandson, and he is staying with me this summer. He has a habit of running away. I don't think having friends right now will do him one bit of good, and . . . I've locked him upstairs." She clamps her jaw shut and opens her eyes wide with a challenge, the way old folks will when they do things no kid could ever get away with.

Theresa actually gasps.

Billy and Georgie are standing on the bench now and edging over to me where I am sitting on one end.

Mrs. Pineroe goes on. "Oh, you needn't be worried. He has every distraction a boy could want up there. And you have my word he does deserve to be there. He'll be going back to his mother later this month and I dare say he'll think twice before running away again." She puts the chain back round her neck, and I see it is a big skeleton key that she has on it. "Or getting up to any of his other shenanigans, for that matter."

Just then the bench stands up from the end where no weight is, and Billy and Georgie pile into me. We fall to the wood floor, and the bench flips and goes crashing, bouncing along the porch.

I'm lying there catching up myself, checking for broken bones and whatnot, when I hear Mrs. Pineroe say, her voice as brittle as an old leaf scratched across concrete, "That will be your menfolk now. Better see them home, missy."

Your face shows your horror and your arms go up and you shake your wrists like something big and scary, and that is **spooky**.

"Well, so much for your ghost," Theresa says to Georgie.

"Can't he still be a ghost?" Georgie asks.

Billy puts his hand up: *Halt.* Then, *What about Rufus?*

"I know, I know," I say. I haven't forgotten. That punched-in-the-gut feeling I got when I first read the dognapping note hasn't gone anywhere. It's just my mind got distracted by Mrs. Pineroe and her keeping her own relative—who we almost thought was a ghost—locked up in her attic like some kind of John Dillinger gangster. "We never said anything about Rufus to her," I say to Theresa.

We are standing in a huddle in the dark outside of the mansion.

"I didn't see any purpose in asking her," Theresa says. "All she knows or cares about is that he's locked up there. Henry, that is."

Instinctively, we swing our heads up to look at the attic window. No light. Billy signs, *I bet he's watching us.* And he waves up at the window. *Bing.* Light goes on.

The silhouette of the boy is there waving back.

We all wave, except Georgie, who is squinting hard.

Then the porch light goes on and the front door opens and out of it comes the voice of Mrs. Pineroe. "Shoo!" she squeaks. "Go home. Right now. I said shoo!"

"We better go before she calls the cops, and she will call them," Theresa says.

We trudge toward the gate and Pineroe Boulevard.

"How come we don't look in the garage?" Georgie asks.

"It's a stable, Georgie. Or it was in its day."

"How come you don't go and see if that Henry boy has Rufus up there for company with his mouth tied shut?"

"Well, I . . ." Theresa's nodding her head. "I . . . we probably will go look. Just not now."

"Why not?"

"Georgie, you want to go to jail?" I say.

"Sure. You mean it?"

"Georgie, you just started school, and already you want to go to jail?"

"I'll go if you'll go, Paolo."

I think Georgie could grow up to be what Sister Alphonsias Ruth Ann calls an "optimist," which, from how she explained it to our class, is kind of like a fool, except you are supposed to want to be one. The way you know you are one is if you go around seeing glasses half full of water. Seems like that would be kind of time-consuming, but optimists are fond of it. And I can see why it is a good kind of stupid 'cause Georgie can make you feel good even when things seem their very worst. "No, Georgie," I say. "Nobody's going to jail. That's why we're leaving."

"You notice there are no dogs barking tonight?" Theresa says.

112

I turn to look at her. "Billy," I say, stopping so he can catch the meaning of my lips, "what do you think?" I'm not asking in order to encourage him. I'm asking 'cause Billy is smarter than any kid his age, and lots who are older, too—he just doesn't believe it on account his teachers don't.

Billy's face is working in the moonlight, and then he signs, *Money. We should get money.*

I think about that and decide the idea has some logic to it, though how much money is anybody's guess.

Theresa is looking back at the tiny square of light at the top of that house, that light like a sign that says, *Don't forget me.* So it's no surprise when she says, "He must be awfully lonely."

"Yeah, ghost or not, it's spooky," I say. "Locked up and all."

"Paolo," Georgie says, "if we can't go to jail, can I have a piggyback?"

"It's too far, Georgie. Besides, you are too big for piggybacks," I say, hands on my hips, frowning down at him.

"But you're my brother."

"What's that got to do with it?"

"Well, you are my manager, too."

Billy gives me a wink that means, *Okay, now what, hotshot?*

I crouch down. "Just get on up and don't say anything."

"I won't say anything at all," Georgie says, wrapping his chubby little fingers, tight, round my throat.

chapter FIFTEEN

Put your index finger next to your right eye and pull the skin into a squint to show the Italian *evil eye*.

Dinner's all finished when we get home. Everyone's up in his or her room or else in the living room listening to the radio. Grandpa and Grandma are gone home. They live over on Terrace Avenue, three blocks away, but drive their Buick over instead of walking 'cause this is America. The only one in the kitchen when we come in the back door is my mom.

She whips her head round and puts her eyes on us like a mother tiger, though she's dark-eyed and dark-haired with skin the color of coffee, not tiger-yellow. She still is young enough to wear her hair down, so it can whip round with her head, not like my grandma, who wears a bun with a little net. First is Georgie, who she makes a quick hard check of for broken bones or bat bites or crying smudges round his eyes or I don't know exactly what. Next, she gives Billy a soft pass and finally bores the evil eye on me.

My mom thinks it's always a possibility that some old Italian lady or other who might have it in for her could put the real evil eye on one of us. (She never thinks it could be her with the eye.) That's why we have to wear a crucifix and a little gold bull's horn round our necks on chains. Even though we got those, she always checks us anyway for signs of the eye. The evil eye can make you shrivel up either slow or quick-like, or catch a cough no doctor can cure. You could also go blind and have to sit in the back pew of San Joaquin Cathedral your whole life like Mr. Tatalino, the bee man. Ernie says it wasn't no evil eye but his own bees that went on strike and stung his eyes blind for his meanness.

She then gives Theresa the same look, though with a faint smile that says something to Theresa in women-talk, until Theresa backs out the door saying, "I'll see you fellows later. Good night, Mrs. O'Neil."

My mom nods. All she says then is "Sit." So we

do, and she serves up zucchini and tomatoes and sausage with fresh sourdough bread from Grandpa's store.

Georgie starts to say something, but Billy and I both shake our heads hard at him, and for once he shuts up and concentrates on his dinner. He starts to chewing and smacking and forgets what he was going to say, though we know it's something about Rufus or Henry or the mansion, all stuff we'd rather not worry Mom with right now.

Mom was raised on a little ranch after my grandpa no longer had to work in the fields but before he got his store, and like I said, she would think of Rufus as a dog—common noun, period. But the idea that someone is sending notes to the house would be a different matter. My mom could go from worry to slashing a switch around the room like Zorro in no time flat. Not that she ever swats us, as we are too fast, and she calms down as quick as she gets mad. Then comes the part that, now that I'm twelve, I like less than any switch—when she clutches us to her and kisses us whilst she has a good cry. I think having all us kids puts an unholy stress on her. Mostly we just try to keep her calm.

Shawna comes in and sits down to watch us, and then after a minute Margarita comes in too. We don't have TV 'cause it's too expensive and on account it irritates my dad. There's just books and the radio and ourselves for distraction, so watching each other eat is an entertainment we enjoy. Italians consider eating more important than baseball, and if they didn't have spaghetti Sunday afternoons at San Joaquin's, I'd bet business would drop off even there.

Betsy must have smelled the cooking 'cause she drifts in too. Seventeen-year-old girls are big on diets and so Betsy can't be blamed for trying to starve herself like she's been pretending to be doing lately. She's the kind of dieter that sits close to you and slips stuff off your plate and pops it into her mouth like it's nothing, like she's just borrowing it for a bit. She's loaned herself enough of my meals in the past few weeks to keep the little pony rump of hers plump. She smiles at me with her soft Appalachian eyes, the sourdough bread of mine she's chewing on a comfort to her I don't really begrudge her having.

Billy blushes when Shawna signs, *Hello, cutie.*

Margarita considers her nails for a while. She keeps them under surveillance for any sign of them cutting into her Italian beauty plans. Then she remembers and says, "Oh, a boy by the name of Butler called to ask where you were this afternoon. You missed your last day to practice with him. Butler said you'd better be at work tomorrow because it's your own paper route now, Paolo."

"But-TER," I correct Margarita. I'm feeling a little guilty about missing our practice work, but I think maybe it's okay 'cause it was for Rufus's sake.

Margarita is not in the habit of being corrected and just passes a plate of butter to me, saying, "You could say please." I let it go, but I give Billy a glare pointing up my displeasure at having a job to worry about. He's not having any of it.

He just shakes his head like, *We're lucky to have one now.*

Margarita says lazily to Shawna, "You know, I saw Mr. Hartoonian at the five-and-dime today, and he showed me a picture of Mike. What a handsome guy. I had no idea."

Shawna says, "I can see that. If Mr. Hartoonian didn't have all that weight, he'd be a very good-looking man."

Betsy doesn't stop her chewing but her eyes

brighten and, cocking her head sideways, she nods in agreement.

I get up from the table then. All women have to do for work is size up a guy and marry him and retire. And here I am already having to get a good night's sleep 'cause, like it or not, I have a *real* job. Tomorrow's Sunday, and that means the one day papers go out in the morning. We have to be up at five o'clock—*a.m.!* On my way out of the kitchen I give Billy and Georgie a little manager's get-to-bed thump on the head, just for good measure.

chapter SIXTEEN

To *discover* is the thumb and forefinger acting like they are picking up something.

Butter has gone to the trouble to make us a list of addresses so we will know which houses to give papers to and which not. He helps us get them folded and loaded and starts to take off just as it's getting light, saying he'll come over to our route when he's finished his. Says it will take us an age the first week, having to stop and check addresses and all. He swats Georgie on the ear when Georgie spits on the ground and accidentally spatters Butter's shoes. Georgie has watched us playing baseball and I think has concluded it's mostly spitting. He's starting to practice.

Actually, it's not shoes, but Butter's engineer

boots he's hit. Butter probably wears that kind 'cause they'll last five years, at least. Well, both Billy and I double our fists, point our right feet out in front of us, facing him like Rocky Marciano, the boxer, our shoulders shrugged forward and our chins tucked, getting ready to unload with our rights. Butter steps back and says, "Man, you'd think that kid was your pet."

Now, that was a curious thing to say, and Billy and I trade a hard look, but I don't spell out our suspicion by speaking. I'm wishing I had that iron right of Rocky's. I've seen him fight on my grandpa's TV on a Friday night. Everybody knows he's going to be the champ.

"All right, all right, now just calm down, okay?" Butter's still backing away. "Lighten up about the kid. I don't suppose you ever thought about the fact that *I'm* helping *you*? You know, I ain't so all-fired happy about having to train you monkeys for nothing. For your information, I happen to need this job." His chubby face is glaring hard with those Oberti olive eyes of his. "I'm only doing this to keep Henderson happy, not you goofs."

He's genuinely mad, and we see how we've taken

him for granted, I guess. But I think he's being a help for the company more than anything. It's Billy that blows air out his nose slowly and then signs, *Sorry*.

"What's that mean?" Butter snorts.

"Means you're right. Just lay off of Georgie. He's a little kid." Georgie, who is behind us, pushes his head in between me and Billy, getting a look. And that's that, because this is work and everything comes second to getting the job done, as we've already seen. Butter takes off, pedaling his bike quickly, shaking his head and talking to himself.

I have the canvas bags on the rack of my Columbia, and Billy has Georgie on the handlebars of his Schwinn. We ride slowly, me weighed down like a pack mule. I have to stand up in my stirrups to move that bike forward. The sky is going from gray to pink, and the clouds on the horizon look like rusty freighters sliding in like I saw once up in Sacramento when we had to visit my aunt Genevieve. Those cloud-ships will be bringing heat and some mugginess, too, no doubt.

When we get to route 408, our route, we have to walk our bikes, me pushing the load and reading the list that I have rubber-banded to my handlebars and

Billy pulling the papers and tossing them onto the porches. When his throws fall short, Georgie runs up and snags them and waddles them to the porch. Those Sunday papers are big, and Georgie looks like he's lugging a big catfish when he does it. He comes back all wet 'cause there's dew on the lawns.

Butter is right. It does take forever, what with not knowing our customers and also the Sunday paper being so heavy. We're actually glad when he shows up before we are even halfway done with our blocks. He helps out without complaining, like nobody is mad about anything, and I guess they aren't. It's eight o'clock when we finish up, our hands and our faces smudged with newsprint ink.

"Come on," Butter says, and starts off on his bike in the direction of downtown. Butter has a way of assuming a guy will do what he says, and it makes a guy do just that. I'd take note of this for my own knowledge 'cept I have no interest in bossing anyone but myself. I remember in third grade when Sister Catherine Agnes said any one of us could grow up to be president, I was worried for a week until I figured out I could be vice president instead and maybe just lounge in my office, not answering the phone if I didn't care to.

Anyway, Butter goes straight to the Downtown Café, sashays in, us following, and lays two papers on the counter.

Mr. Weinchek, the owner, pulls a jelly doughnut from the top of these little glass bleachers inside a glass case and drops it in a white paper bag and hands it to Butter. Georgie asks if he can have a jelly doughnut too. Mr. Weinchek looks the whole of us over and takes the white bag from Butter's hands and slips three more doughnuts into it. "Just this once," he says to Butter, who nods and then gives Georgie a glare until he catches me and Billy giving him our best idea of the Italian evil eye.

Then we ride over to Butter's house and go in the front door. His mom must be asleep 'cause there is no one around. Butter won't let us in to any rooms but the living room and a little dining room. He spreads another newspaper all round the floor and lays out the doughnuts. He goes in the kitchen and comes back with a bottle of milk. Says there aren't any clean glasses and we can just drink straight from the bottle. We nod at that, appreciating the luxury Butter has of having no dad and a mom who is distracted.

Then Butter turns the RCA on and dials up the comics. In Orange Grove the kids from the high school dramatics club read the comics every Sunday morning. They make all the voices and the sounds, like a whomp! or the click-click-click of high heels or whatever is needed. We know about it but never have had the paper to go along with the voices before and are all lined up on the floor with our hands on our chins and propped up on our elbows, eyes tracing the color pictures. I use my finger, too, so Georgie knows what's going on, though he can read some on his own. Butter sits in a recliner with a huge tear in the upholstery, his feet up, watching us and nodding with satisfaction.

When it's over, we roll on our backs, impressed with the show. Georgie falls to sleep, and even Billy looks drowsy. I yawn.

"Tired, huh?" Butter says to me.

"Yeah, but I don't feel bad."

"That's because you're work-tired. Wait till you get paid. Feels even better."

Butter is an interesting sort, and I almost think he could be a friend, but I know not to make friends all that quick. Besides, with my family, I don't hardly need friends. Besides, on account of his strangeness and his being jealous of us and Georgie, Butter's a suspect.

"Butter," I say, "could you show me again how that receipt book works?"

"Sure," he says, and goes to the dining room table and fetches it, comes back, and waves me over. I go and we sit there, and he shows me where to put the customers' names and where to put mine and where the date goes and everything. Of course, I know it all already and am studying his writing. And, yes, he writes in little looping letters.

chapter SEVENTEEN

Make a **C** shape out of your right hand and tap it on the back of your left hand. That's a stone, the rock that is Peter on which Jesus built his *church*.

If you got a guy under your suspicion, you don't want him knowing it. I get Butter to give me one of his old receipts, telling him I will use it as an example but really so's I can check it next to the dognapping note. Thing is, Theresa must still have that note from the day I showed it to her 'cause I don't have it anywhere. For once I figure I will have to call her up.

But all that has to wait 'cause it's Sunday, and it's the Sunday that is Billy's and my turn to serve Mass. I wake him up, as he's fallen asleep along with Georgie on Butter's floor, Georgie's head in Billy's armpit and Billy's elbow slung round Georgie's head like a soft headlock. We leave, carrying Georgie between us, Butter standing in his doorway waving us away like he's President Teddy Roosevelt and we're his Rough Riders about to gallop off with one of our dead after doing a good job.

I am trying to use the straps from my canvas bags to tie Georgie to Billy's handlebars to keep him from falling off when he wakes up, sees the straps, and starts howling. It takes me a couple of minutes to convince him I ain't kidnapping him like somebody dognapped Rufus. I have to tell him that you get the electric chair for kidnapping and I have no intention of getting flash-cooked or even chancing it, and besides, he would tell on us when we traded him back to my folks, wouldn't he? That makes sense to him, I guess, 'cause he calms down and lets us get him home.

Billy and I wash all that newsprint from ourselves and put on our Sunday white shirts and slap Old Spice all over each other. We don't have time for a proper bath, and besides, we'd already had ours last night, as it was Saturday. We bike on down to San Joaquin's just in time for the eleven o'clock service. We hustle up quick, pulling our gear on. We get to wear either these long red or black dress sort of things—called "vestments"—and 'cause it's summer, we wear the red. We put big white blouses on over everything. When we are done, we look like angels ready for bed with nightshirts on, which is the general idea, I think.

We get out front on stage and light the candles with this six-foot-long cigarette lighter that I'd trade anything to have, and then we go get Monsignor.

Monsignor is in the back in his room waiting on us and praying, which he can do whilst snoring just this very little bit. We have to poke him two or three times to get him to break off talking silently to the Lord, as is his habit.

Monsignor is Irish. Bald and short and red in the face—red as Billy when he's sunburned—with veins trickling everywhere. He has a fondness for wine that's normal for him. He's a genuine priest and a help to most and so hasn't got one enemy in Orange Grove, which is good. Ernie says even the cops like the Monsignor well enough that they will stop him at night and make him leave his car right where it is just so's they can chauffeur him home out of respect. I guess it makes him feel like a king 'cause he lets them keep doing it, even though he has to walk to get his car every morning.

We get Monsignor going and the Mass starts on time. Mostly there is nothing for us to do except kneel, looking at Monsignor. About the only thing that would get you fired from being an altar boy is staring at folks in the audience or waving to your friends. You'd have to be stupid to do that, as you can see everyone when it comes time for Communion, when you hold the little gold plate under their chins.

I was going to be a dentist till I got a look in people's mouths. All fleshy and pink and that little wiggly bit in the back of their throats, bad breath and teeth looking like little mushrooms crowding up from the dirt. Tongues waving at you. It puts a chill on me, so mostly I close my eyes and imagine I'm praying. Billy makes sure the gold plate goes under the chins in the right spot.

Everybody is there, as usual. All my family and half the kids from school, even Rodney Paul and Theresa. Not Butter, 'cause he's churched up elsewhere, I guess, or doesn't go. And up comes Mrs. Pineroe. I'd seen her lots of times, just didn't know who she was in particular. And right on her heels is a boy about ten or eleven in a blue blazer and blue button-down shirt. Hair white as cotton, skin scrubbed raw, and hard butterscotch eyes. He's got one arm hanging by his side and one in the pocket of his jacket, and just before he gets to the altar rail, he takes that hand out and holds it to the other like he's praying. And one of those hands is shriveled up with the fingers curled back in a little otter's claw. And my mouth is dropped open with wonder when Henry smiles and gives a little snort like he's about to laugh, then gives me a wink, just as jolly as you please.

chapter EIGHTEEN

The thumb of your open hand taps the side of your forehead to mean a *dad*.

Billy and I stop by Russ Mueller's on our way home. Russ Mueller's Gas, Oil & Lube is the oldest gas station in Orange Grove City, I bet. Used to be out in the fig orchards, but now it's not far from downtown on a street with big old houses and a center divider that has grass and giant Christmas trees growing.

We go inside, where Mr. Mueller is sitting at the window of his little metal hut. He's reading the paper. Looks up. He's redheaded and skin-spotted, 'cause he's Theresa's dad. We don't have nickels, so we aren't outside with our arms up to their elbows in ice water getting our sodas as usual. "Mr. Mueller, we need to talk to Theresa, and I don't have her phone number," I say.

Mr. Mueller snaps his paper, turns the page, and lays it on his desk, then smoothes it flat, real slow, with both hands. Looks up at me with Theresa's runny-water eyes. "Well, Paolo, you are just the man I wanted to see. In fact, I was thinking of calling *you*."

Now, I'm not stupid. Nobody has to call you for something good. No one calls you to open presents on Christmas; no one calls you to go get the baseball equipment at recess. They call you to come back from recess or to take a bath or the like.

"Well, what is it you wanted to call about?" I ask, 'cause Mr. Mueller hasn't said and is trying some kind of mind torture by not saying. I was trained by the best, so I'm not worried . . . yet. I say, offhand and pleasant, "Mr. Mueller, you know I can get you a deal on your newspaper if you like. You are probably paying a quarter on Sundays, right?"

Mr. Mueller frowns, unhappy I'm all cheery.

"I'll hook you up with a paper every Sunday for two Nehi root beers."

He latches on to that. "Two, huh? One for you and one for Billy?"

I begin to nod when he cuts me short, quick.

"Or is it one for Theresa?" Now his blood is up, I can tell, 'cause his ears are getting red as the reddest of bell peppers.

"Theresa could get one for free anytime," I say in the softest voice ever, my eyes falling away.

"That's right, Paolo, she could, and she doesn't need you pulling her all over town night and day. Do you hear me?"

I want to tell him Theresa does all the pulling and, as far as I'm concerned, she's as much fun as measles and about as pretty as he his. But he's her dad, and he's not going to believe any of that. I used to wonder why there were ugly kids in the world until I saw their parents. It was a revelation to me 'cause I saw that there was never any need to worry if you were handsome or otherwise 'cause ugly folks find one another all the time and get married without any trouble. And, also, I know that it is entirely possible that Theresa is one of those girls Ernie told me about—the kind that aren't as ugly as they look. But I don't say any of this, just keep my head bowed.

"All right, I'm glad we've had this little talk, then."

Now I am glad too, as it solves my being bothered

anymore by Theresa, but I still need to see that dognapping note.

"Okay, you can go," says Mr. Mueller. He doesn't seem mad anymore. He's usually real friendly.

Billy opens the door, and we are standing at it when I say, "It's nice how Theresa looks out for her grandma. Spends all Sunday there and everything." Then I watch his face to see if I'm right.

That face darkens and the ears light up and start pulsing. "She does, and if anyone was to disturb her, they'd be very sorry," he says. That's what his words say, but his voice says, all flayed like a dried fish, *I am prepared to break your arms and legs and drown you in the sink right out back here.*

Dads are crazy about their daughters. Grandpas, too. Grandpa Leonardo says we are to take sticks to any boy that even talks to our sisters. But two of my sisters have boyfriends. Margarita has Jimmy Assayian, who let me crash his car once giving me driving lessons, and Shawna has Terence Gaston the Third, who fished Georgie out of the ditch where he was getting ready to drown. I haven't seen those two lately, but I think it's luck my sisters got them 'cause that's two that won't need more supporting if everything goes well. I understand why the dad has to give a party when a girl gets a fellow to marry her.

What I don't get is why they marry them in the first place. Ernie told me it's like girls have a kind of fairy dust they carry and powder you down with when you aren't looking, and then you think every little thing about them is precious. The way they burp even will make you smile to think on. My hand goes up to touch the crucifix round my neck at the thought.

"Yes, sir" is all I say to Mr. Mueller, and head out the door. We know that since we can't go and see Theresa, we can't compare Butter's handwriting on the receipt to the dognapping note. I decide that the only thing we can do next, then, is check out Henry and maybe his stable. That way we can rule him in or out as the dognapper.

Billy and I are walking away when Mr. Mueller calls to us from the doorway. "You can bring the paper next Sunday, okay?" He's being buddy-buddy again. All just-between-guys.

I nod and Billy gives him a weak wave. We should be happy, as we just got our first off-the-books customer, but we're not.

If you want to say **brothers**, or those you think of as part of your **brotherhood**, close your fists but leave the thumbs out. Put one hand above the other—one thumb down, one up—and circle your hands, like they are tumbling over and over each other.

At nine p.m. on Sundays it's lights-out at our house. My dad goes round and switches off any that might be left on, saying just 'cause Ernie works for Pacific Gas & Electric, we aren't responsible for his salary. He even shuts the cooler down on nights we could use the breeze. We are lying in our beds, a little mist of sweat on us, waiting to hear my mom go to bed. Mom does ironing at night, uses this big old professional ironer that is like two bread dough rollers the size of small logs. She rolls the clothes through them, wringing them and ironing them flat and then steaming them, too. All the controls are like an organ's—at your feet and one is right next to your knee; that one you press sideways to clamp the rollers together. When she first got it, secondhand from Janian's Dry Cleaning, all of us helped out with the ironing for a whole week. Anyway, we hear that thing sigh with the last of its steam, and she comes upstairs to her room, where my dad is already asleep.

We snap out of our beds like rubber bands that have been held tight near to breaking for half an hour and get our gear—twenty feet of clothesline, a flashlight, a Swiss Army knife, a blindfold, Hector's old slingshot, seventy-two specially picked rocks for ammunition. We have it all in a pillowcase. Georgie is going too, 'cause he's awake this time and we'd have to duct tape him to his bed if we left him. There wasn't any duct tape in the garage when Billy and I checked after we got home from Russ Mueller's and hatched our plan to investigate Henry. Regular rope wouldn't do, as Georgie is little and squirmy and can get free. Well, he's got loose any time in the past we've tried it. He has a special talent that way and may even get to work in the circus when he grows up, for all I know.

Billy climbs out the window. Georgie has to be lowered to Billy with the clothesline by me. Takes five minutes just to do it. I have the glow-in-the-dark Timex wristwatch Grandpa gave me last year on my birthday, so I know. Georgie's loving every minute of it to the point that makes me almost start laughing out loud. I decide I'm glad of him in spite of his being a relative I have to look out for all the time.

We are still making our way down the side of the house when up the driveway come two headlights climbing the outside of the house then swinging round the yard, stabbing the darkness. It's Ernie turning into the driveway in his '41-'42 Ford convertible that we know he just bought. Its big V-8 engine rumbles up and shuts down and the headlamps go off and the car glides silently up the drive, then stops right where Billy and I have jumped into the bushes, Billy's hand slapped over Georgie's mouth. That car counts for two years 'cause somebody bolted the '41 part with the engine and stuff to the '42 part where the steering wheel and the seats and the rest is. The front end is black primer and the back is white.

Actually, that car is Ernie's *and* Hector's, just like everything else they own. They have in their time bought an old BMW motorcycle that ran sometimes, a subscription to *Boxing World,* a king snake they kept in a glass box, a heavily rusted shotgun, and a water pipe they still use to smoke in the garage, bubbling and coughing and talking like sultans about karate and car mufflers and the advantages of not paying taxes.

Ernie wouldn't mind our sporting on a summer night, but it's the fact that he's got a girl with him that has us off balance and hiding. She's mostly shadow and scooted all close to him with her fingers clamped round the back of his head like a deepwater sea creature. Even fifteen feet away, I can smell her lavender perfume. Hear the little wet smacking sounds I know is kissing. The weird part is, Ernie pulls away every little bit and baby-talks at her. Never heard that, though he'd warned me that when you get to talking like a baby to a girl, you are a goner and certifiably out of your mind and in need of a keeper. Knowing the danger, I remember the Bible and feel a rush of brotherly love for him, and realize I will have to be the keeper and make myself known to save him.

I open my mouth to shout when Billy pinches it shut. I'm shocked and look sideways at him, wide-eyed.

I see he's got Georgie in a headlock with his mouth clamped tight too. Georgie's feet are off the ground and his legs are scissoring slow like he's drowning; like I said, Billy's other hand is stapling my lips together. He gives me a look that says, *Keep quiet and I'll let go.*

I relax, and he lets loose of me and then points to the car. I touch my mouth that is still smarting and follow the line of his pointing and see that there in the backseat is Hector, sitting upright and still as a cigar-store Indian. Then I know that Ernie is safe and one step ahead of everybody, like he always is. I feel the air fade out of me in relief and shake my head in wonder and find that I'm again hoping truly I have the same smarts somewhere in me—that they will show themselves soon so I can find Rufus, though I might have to get a little more time on this earth with all its mysteries before that happens.

chapter TWENTY

If something is really **weird**, and you want to make note of it, just take three fingers and make a **W**, fingers pointing up, and bounce them across the front of your nose.

Soon enough we are standing in the bushes right next to the mansion. I'm going to climb up to the little attic window—looks like its own little house sticking out from the roof—to talk to Henry. We already checked for Rufus in the stable, and nothing was there except some mice and a few pigeons that exploded up out into the night through a hole in the roof when we turned on the flashlight to look things over.

Georgie will stay under the big redwood in the bushes as a lookout. There is nobody to look out for—me and Billy can hear and see for ourselves— but we tell Georgie it's an important job so he doesn't go wandering and get lost or pecked to death by peacocks. Anyway, he's agreeable. And excited— though a little sleepy.

Billy and I are able to climb that tree faster than we did the first time. I make the big step from the branches to the edging under the attic and slide myself over, my back to the face of the house, until I'm right underneath that attic window-box thing that juts out. Billy has the sack with all our gear minus the rope and blindfold, which I have hanging from my belt. On my cue Billy loads up the smallest pebble into our slingshot and shoots it in a soft arc to Henry's window. It doesn't break the glass or even make a tapping sound. Instead, I hear chuckling, and I realize the window is open and Henry's right there watching us.

That makes me mad, and I am about to tell him that I'm going to come in there and give him a beating when he says, "Here, give me your arm and I'll swing you up."

I don't know why I trust him, except that his voice sounds sincere and 'cause when I had a look at him at church, he seemed okay enough for a little rich kid. I hope he's going to grab me with the regular hand, not the little otter claw. I sling my arm up, hooking it inside the window frame, and Henry pulls me up slick as you please. We stand there in the dark breathing heavily.

"I'm Henry," he says in a rough little frog voice, nervous-like, not like the voice he just used a minute before.

"Paolo," I say.

"Should we get the boy who doesn't talk up here too?" he asks with that gravelly voice again that makes him sound scared of me. Sounds the way some kids' voices get when they have to give a speech in school. Like all the spit has dried out on account they are embarrassed.

"Billy? He can't quite make that big step from the tree to the edging."

"I know." Henry giggles, like he's just forgotten to be nervous, his voice smooth as can be all of a sudden. "I have a plank I pulled out from up in the rafters yesterday." He disappears for a minute and comes back with a short, sturdy board.

The notion seems kind of dicey to me. "I don't know," I say.

"I do," Henry says. "I've measured it. I can't make that step myself, but if . . . if . . ."

"Billy?" I ask.

"Yes. If Billy puts his end in tight to the tree and with that rope of yours around him and us on this end, it will be a snap." And he snaps his fingers. He's an optimist, I can tell.

Well, it isn't a snap. But we do get Billy into Henry's attic, after some fair bit of struggle. Once he's there, Henry falls onto his back and uses one foot to push himself round in circles whilst slapping his good hand on the floor with delight. In the dark and the moonlight he looks like a madman's shadow that's escaped its owner and come alive of its own. Suddenly, he sits up. "Fellows, you know what this means?"

We just look at his dark self until I ask, "Can we turn on some lights or something?"

"Sure!" he says. Jumps up and switches on a little table lamp that's on a miniature desk next to the window. It's a lamp that has a plastic cylinder that stands upright with a light inside and turns in a slow circle, these pictures of tropical fish casting watery shadows that waver round the whole room. I see Billy is still sweating from our labor or from the fright he got walking that board. Then Henry is there in our faces. "It means, my dear friends, that if Billy can get in, I can get out. Ha-ha!"

"Well, that's great, Henry, but . . . *we* have some questions for you."

Billy nods his head.

"Questions?" Henry squeaks. "I love questions. I love answers even more." He sounds like one crazy, troublesome peacock or . . . well, I don't even know what. Maybe he's been locked up too long.

Billy pulls the desk chair out and sits down, his arm over the back of it, his legs crossed like a man—a school principal or something. I notice there is a telescope on a stand right there by the window. Henry is still saying stuff like questions and answers, yes, questions and answers, when I squint into it and start swinging it around. I can see lights from a mile or more back in Orange Grove, even pick out the blinking neon bucking horse over Western Liquors. I wonder about Georgie and dial him up with my giant eye. He's right there below, flat on his back, face as big as a casaba melon in the moonlight, and asleep now—no surprise. For a kid as little as Georgie, the middle of the night is really the middle of the night. I turn my attention to Henry. In the light I see he's in pajamas with cowboys chasing cows all round himself. We don't own pajamas in our house except for the girls. We sleep in our Fruit of the Looms.

"You have the questions now, right?" Henry says happily.

I just can't get a handle on this kid. Except it's obvious he's his own style of strange. If his mind were a house, it would be haunted.

"Sit down," I say.

He immediately drops to the floor, sitting cross-legged, looking up, blinking those big candy-yellow eyes, his hair like corn silk roughed this way and that. I can't understand how he has a tan whilst locked in the way he's been.

I look at Billy. He gets up and comes to stand next to me. He takes the slingshot out and loads it with the biggest of our rocks. He pulls back and aims it at Henry. Billy is a gentle one, but he can be mean if he gets a notion he wants to be.

I say, "You know anything about our dog?"

Henry is looking at the slingshot and at Billy's face and then mine, and he starts sniffling, puts his little claw hand to his eye.

Billy lowers the slingshot.

Henry immediately smiles. "I don't have a dog, so I don't have my dog, so I don't have your dog—or our dog. My aunt doesn't have a dog, my mother would never have a dog, and I don't really know if I'd want her to have one, actually. She doesn't even enjoy having me. Maybe she would, though, if I were a dog." His eyes mist up at that thought. Like his mind is sucking on the sadness of himself and trying to get after every bit of that poison—sort of the way, in the third grade, Vincent Velasco would get after candy even though his teeth were all rotted. Henry sticks his lower lip out like Georgie, except it ain't flattering for a boy who's maybe ten or more.

Billy is frowning.

Henry's a kooky one, what my grandpa would call "kookamunga," but he does seem honest as a nun. I don't think he has a clue about Rufus. But maybe he's crazy and doesn't know what he's done or not.

Billy signs to me, *What do you think is the matter with his hand?*

I shrug. Shriveled. Like he'd been evil-eyed for real, I think. Henry catches us looking at that little back-curled hand of his. He says, quiet now, almost a whisper, "I had polio when I was little.

It's a sickness. Gives you fevers and makes you paralyzed. Some people die, and some are just left with a part of themselves like this." He holds up the shrunk hand.

"Is it catching?" I blurt out without thinking. I know that isn't polite to ask, but the truth is, I guess I do not want little fish flippers for hands. It's natural to fear such a thing.

"It is when you have the fever and all, but that was years ago."

"Sorry," I say, not knowing what else to say, and I am sorry he has to go through life with that affliction. I look at Billy, but he doesn't sign anything or say anything with his eyes, either. Maybe he understands Henry on account he has his own affliction. But it must be something else, too, 'cause he's just looking at Henry's hand and then at his face and back again, trying to figure something out I don't know.

To *listen* is your hand cupping an ear
to hear better.

We end up talking to Henry for half the night. He
tells us that he runs away 'cause his mother is
divorced and spends all her time giving her attentions
to boyfriends. Billy listens hard with his eyes to that
part. Henry says he once stole thirty-seven dollars
from one of those boyfriends to buy a bus ticket to
Alaska but never got farther than Seattle, where two
policemen in regular clothes took him off the bus. So
it's my turn to listen hard, I guess. I ask how much it
costs to get all the way to Alaska, but he doesn't
know. I still have my hankering to go to Alaska like
Mike Hartoonian did, a hankering to try out a part of
the world other than Orange Grove. Not that I don't
like it here, as I do, but going to a place where all is

151

wild seems a thing worth doing. I think Henry is not so crazy.

He says nobody likes him because of his hand, but he's used to that. Says his great-aunt, Mrs. Pineroe, is too old to be taking him for the summer and should never have locked him in his room, but he isn't going to report her to the police or anything 'cause she's just too old to know what to do with a guy his age— ten years old. This is the first time we hear just exactly what his age is.

She locked him up the second day he was here after he'd gone into town and come back courtesy of the cops because he was sitting at a bus stop watching the ladies out front of the Sequoia Hotel at eleven-thirty at night. Says all he was doing was asking them their names 'cause he was curious to see if all of them would have the names of pastries like the first two he'd asked—Sweet Cake and Muffin. Also, Billy and I find out that what Mrs. Pineroe and Henry call "all summer" is only three weeks.

When Henry talks, sometimes his voice will go gravelly, roughed up and nervous for a bit, then back excited to the point of kooky. I listen hard, and not just to the words, but what might be under the words to see why and where his voice changes but can't tell.

I tell him—Billy nodding as I go along—all about our trouble with Rufus, and that seems of genuine excitement to him. After I tell him, he walks round his room thinking and holding up his hand for silence every time I'm about to add something and ducking his head when he gets to the sloped-down parts of the ceiling. Then he spins toward us and says, "Butter is your man. From what you are saying, he hasn't a friend in the world. He's either jealous or he thinks you will have to come to him to help find your dog." He says it like he knows himself about what lonesomeness might make a guy do. He leans forward and whispers, "And the trick is going to be catching him in the act."

"The act . . . of what?" I ask.

"Feeding your dog, taking care of him . . . unless Rufus is dead, and I certainly hope that isn't so." He looks at me. Comes right over and stares into my eyes. "Do you *feel* as if Rufus is dead?"

"No," I say, though I do feel funny putting any much stock in what could be the kookamunga notions of a kid who has to be locked in an attic.

"Billy?" Henry looks over at him.

Billy shakes his head.

"Neither do I."

"Why exactly would Butter do it? Say that part again," I ask.

"Well, you said it yourself."

"I did?"

"The stuff you said about how he treats Georgie. Remember that? He's jealous. Not everyone has ready-made friends like you do with your big family. And if you have to go to him to help you find Rufus, you'll have to be his friend."

"But he already gets to hang around us, showing us the paper route."

"Yeah, but that's almost over, right?"

"Yeah, and maybe *you* wanted to get us to come over here to be your friends. Maybe you have a way to get in and out of here without us helping you." I don't think I really believe that, but I don't want Henry believing he's the only one who thinks.

"Aw, c'mon, guys. Let's catch this Butter boy," he says. And his eyes shine.

Make the sign for *girl* (see chapter 13) and then clasp your hands together to show *marry*. *Girl + marry = wife.*

"He's still in bed," says Alice-Ann to my ten-year-old sister and her own twin, Aurora.

"Just like him," says Aurora.

"Should we leave him alone?"

I groan and roll over in my bed to face them where they are standing in the doorway. Pillow clamped over my ears. Alice-Ann puts her pigtailed head on Aurora's shoulders, closes her eyes, and starts making choking and strangling and snoring noises.

Alice-Ann and Aurora's latest invention is to talk to folks as if those persons weren't in the room—to say *he* instead of *you* and the like. As their ambition in life is to be annoying to older brothers, they are pleased pink with their new sport.

It's got to be the next day. I sit up and see Billy and Georgie are already up and gone. We left Henry last night with the agreement we'd come get him in the afternoon in time for our paper route so he can try out his ideas for catching Butter doing something that'll give him away as Rufus's snatcher.

"His girlfriend is on the phone."

"What does she see in him?"

The two of them are so skinny that they suddenly remind me of Popeye's wife standing next to her reflection in a mirror.

"He's awake."

"He'll come down to the phone."

They spin on their heels like soldiers and march off.

I throw off the sheets and pull on my Levi's and T-shirt and pad quickly downstairs and pick up the phone. "Hello?"

"Hi, Paolo. I'm just calling you to see how you are. I didn't see you yesterday, except at church."

"Uh-huh."

"There just isn't anything to *do*," Theresa says.

"Yeah . . ."

"What would you do if you were totally bored, Paolo?"

After a bit where I'm rubbing my eyes, I say, "Sit around thinking up the most fascinating person I knew and then call them on the telephone."

Silence.

Then Theresa snaps back, "Oh, and why not the most egotistical person you've ever met?"

"Because that person isn't a guy," I say.

And then something odd happens. Theresa starts giggling, and then . . . I do, too. Alice-Ann and Aurora have slipped into the room and have their backs to me with their hands wrapped busily around the rear of their heads and their shoulders like they are being kissed by well-trained mechanics, guys good with their hands.

I turn away and shut my eyes 'cause they keep peeking to see if they are having any effect on me. "Say, Theresa, you still have that dognapping note?" I whisper into the phone. "I need to see if it matches Butter's writing." Seems to me Theresa has forgotten that what's important is finding Rufus.

"I'm sure I do. Somewhere. I can find it."

"I'd really like to have a look at it."

"Great, can you come here? I'm at my grand-mother's now, watching her."

"Your dad anywhere around there?"

"No, he's at the station."

"'Cause he forbade me to be near you."

"Oh, silly, my dad says all kinds of stuff."

"Yeah? I kind of got the impression he meant it."

"Don't be such a scaredy-cat. Come on over." And she hangs up.

It's seven blocks to Theresa's house, then a bit farther to her grandmother's. I am taking my time, wondering what it would be like to be drowned in the tub Mr. Mueller keeps back of his place that he uses to check for leaks in inner tubes. I'm walking since it is only eleven o'clock and there's time to get Henry and then Butter and do our routes this afternoon and what else we have to do. Theresa's grandma lives where the houses thin out—folks having an acre or more to themselves—until there are no houses at all and the long yellow grass and jackrabbit heaven begins.

Ernie told me he and Hector hunted rabbits once. Said they were both excellent shots. Either one of them could get off ten rounds in under a minute. Said they could have got a lot of those rabbits if only they didn't have such sensitive ears. After being shot at for some time, they just disappeared underground. To get away from all the racket.

Suddenly, I hear air brakes hissing, shunting down; I turn, and there's Mr. Hartoonian in the biggest truck I've ever seen him drive. He's got a helper in the cab too. Johnny Liston, a guy so sharp-like and skinny, he looks as if he could be made out of bamboo. Got a head like a cantaloupe. Reminds me of Timothy Schroeder's. Timothy's head is so small that in football no helmet will fit him. Has to tape newspapers all round his head, and still when he gets hit, that helmet shoots off like a champagne cork.

Mr. Hartoonian leans out his window and says, "Need a ride, Paolo?"

I wouldn't mind one, especially in that truck, but don't feel like being squished between Mr. Hartoonian and his helper. It'd be like the hard fork of Johnny squeezing me into the mashed potatoes of Mr. Hartoonian.

"Nah, but thanks anyway."

"Well, don't be in such a rush. You want the sports section?"

"No. Got my own route now," I say.

"No kidding. Well, whatta ya know." He raises his eyebrows and says, "Wanna see something?"

I look at him, his arm out the window like a calf's leg hanging down.

"Come on," he says.

I climb onto the running board and pull myself up by the chrome bars of the big truck mirrors. Mr. Hartoonian is fumbling open a letter. "Right here, Paolo," he says, pointing a fat finger at a line of that letter. He reads, slowly, three words at a time: "'Dad, if you / won't come up / here, I may / just have to / come down there / to see you. / But you should / come up here. / I have seen / Orange Grove, but / you have never / seen anything like / my little cabin.'" He finishes, his eyes gleaming.

Johnny snorts loudly. "Why don't you go on up there next Christmas? You could hitch a ride with Santa coming back."

Mr. Hartoonian quickly folds the letter and slips it into the front pocket of his work shirt. He looks at me. "You think I should go visit?"

Johnny is rolling his eyes.

"Uh . . . sure. Absolutely, Mr. Hartoonian. Heck, I'll go with you. Billy would too."

Mr. Hartoonian blinks at that. "Well, well, I'd—I would probably go alone. If I was to actually go."

"If he was to go," echoes that Johnny, head back over his seat, eyes closed. "If there was someone to actually visit up there."

"We'll see you around, Paolo," Mr. Hartoonian says, getting steamed. I know now why he won't show anyone that envelope's postmark, 'cause I've asked Ernie. He explained that it is a matter of pride. Mr. Hartoonian probably feels by now that he shouldn't have to prove anything to anyone, Ernie said with a wink, or he has made the whole thing up.

Mr. Hartoonian guns the motor once, pops it in gear, and stutters out of there, huffing diesel. I watch the truck climb through its gears and rumble on until it disappears in the heat squiggles coming off of the two-lane running out into the country.

"Paolo!"

I look, and there is Theresa standing under a big mulberry planted close to the street. She's holding up a lady with an old newspaper-yellow complexion and a Pepto-Bismol-pink dress. Has to be her grandma. There isn't any sidewalk here, and Theresa looks like she needs help balancing the old lady. I go over quickly to them. Take Mrs. Mueller's other arm. "Nice to meet you, ma'am," I say.

"Nice to see you, too, Russ."

"She gets mixed up," Theresa says, as if her grandma can't hear.

"Are you supposed to take her on the road?" I ask. She looks to me like one strong puff of wind could blow out her candle for good.

"Well, not exactly. But, seriously, Paolo . . ." Theresa's eyes are suddenly lacquered slick with hurt. "If you never knew when would be the last time you might be able to go out-of-doors, wouldn't you want to go? Want someone to take you?" Theresa's mouth is crinkling this way and that. I think about what it would be like if my grandparents were sick. But, also, I notice Theresa has a new sundress on. Bloodred roses spilling down it. Bare arms. My noticing that should scare me, but it doesn't.

We are standing in the cool of the tree. Whoever owns the acre has most of it growing lawn grass, which isn't the usual. Most out here have a little corral or some fig or orange trees out front of their house. This is like a little park.

"Here, help me sit her down," Theresa says.

We place Grandma Mueller gently on the grass, stooping down with all the care that we have. Then we sit together with her to one side.

"I haven't been to a picnic since we left Michigan. Before you were born, Russ," Mrs. Mueller says.

"Oh, Grandma, we went on a picnic just last month."

"Oh, yes, that's right, isn't it?" She's looking right into Theresa's eyes and lying her head off like a kid. She doesn't remember any picnic, you can tell. Then she looks at me. "Who is your boyfriend here?"

Theresa brightens a little with embarrassment, but it gets her off of being so sad. "This is my friend Paolo."

"Anyone ever tell you, you look a lot like my boy, Russ."

"Yeah, lately, all the time."

Mrs. Mueller giggles, and I laugh too. I'm starting to like her myself. It's too bad some kids don't think much of old folks. Just 'cause they can't do a jump shot or hit a homer doesn't mean they aren't of use. I think they are the ones most likely to take a genuine interest in you.

"Mrs. Mueller, how old were you when you had

your first boyfriend?" I'm asking to tease Theresa a little and also as it has occurred to me that I want to know.

"Seven. Can't recall his name. He was Michael Wheeler's friend."

"That's the second grade," I say. Mrs. Mueller's got a wild look in her eye just remembering. Women *are* dangerous.

"Of course, he didn't figure it out for a long time. I must have bumped into him a hundred times, and all he thought was that I was clumsy or in need of spectacles. 'Course, that man was never very bright."

"How long did it take him to catch on?"

"Oh, sometime after Russ was born."

My mouth is a railroad tunnel, dark and wide.

Theresa smiles, grateful, I think, that I don't think nothin' about her having a grandma that's a bit touched. Theresa gets stuck looking at me. I can't really fault her for that, but, finally, I stand up and motion her over with me to the other side of the tree from her grandma.

Theresa stands slowly, leaning down to straighten the collar of her grandma's dress who's looking round like everything's new—the grass, the sky, and the gnats. She watches Theresa stand up, then figures out nobody is going anywhere and goes back to looking at things, distracted. Then Theresa steps over to me where I'm standing now behind the tree.

I whisper, "Can I see the dognapping note?"

"Oh, shoot." Theresa's eyes are now a splash of cold brook water. "I forgot to run home and look for it. But I will, Paolo. Don't be disappointed." I see she has some little bit of makeup on, and I don't think it hurts her any. Now it's me that's just looking at her, not saying anything. Instead of thinking of Rufus's note, I'm wondering what it would feel like to touch that skin of her arms. I want to know how girl skin is different from boy's. I got a sudden case of what my dad calls the "I-want-to-knows."

Grandma's babbling something in the background. I snatch a quick peek round the tree at her. She's sitting there ten yards from us, talking to a squirrel that looks to be a country squirrel, not one to come very close, even if Mrs. Mueller is talking sweet to it and holding out her hand like she's got something for it.

Theresa says, her whole self a soft whisper, "It's nice, here in the shade." She shivers. I'm still taken by her skin and taken by the fact that it is of such interest to me when suddenly it occurs to me maybe her body is just a smooth shape to keep her quivering in and that it's really her heart, which is big, that is doing the quivering. It's a new thought for me, and I'm trying to get my mind around it.

While I'm staring and thinking and probably looking like an idiot, she leans against me and stretches her neck up and kisses me right on the lips. Just a little peck. I don't do anything. She looks me in the eyes, then closes them and kisses me again. And believe me, it isn't as bad as it sounds, 'cause at that minute I'm out of my mind, I guess. But the truth is, *I kiss back.*

chapter

Middle finger and forefinger make the V shape; curl the V back, bending it, and then touch the lips to ***whistle***.

Well, I haven't walked but ten feet away from Theresa, far enough so her fairy dust can't reach me anymore, I guess, because without even thinking, I turn around slowly as if remembering and say, "On account of your dad, you have to stay away from me."

Color drops right out of her face. Shock is like milk splashed across it. She pivots, goes back to the other side of the tree, her back to me, starts fiddling with her grandma's dress, adjusting it or something, Grandma's head bobbling, weak. I think Theresa is hiding her crying. Or cussing.

I go on and leave, and the truth is, while I walk, I think that if things get out of control, at least Theresa goes to the same church as us, so there won't be any need of her converting, though I wonder what big, red Russ Mueller would look like stuffed into a wedding tux. Think about how I'd have to ask Dad if we could live in his garage for a while, maybe sleep in our Chevy station wagon, at least till I finished junior high. But by the time I meet up with Billy and Georgie on the back porch of our house, Theresa doesn't seem so huge and important. I'm grateful. My mom has given them our lunch in a grocery sack.

It's only a ten-minute bicycle ride to work, and going there, working, and getting back home is only a two-hour job, but Italians do not travel without food. Mom doesn't always remember, but when she does, she'll do like today—make batter-fried eggplant and summer pepper sandwiches on sourdough bread. We'll be home before we are hungry, but to my mom we are Lewis and Clark setting out to discover America. Once when we went to the coast for the day, my dad had to rent a trailer to haul all the cooking gear she wanted.

Billy and Georgie and I eat the sandwiches right there on the back steps, as it is too much of a bother to carry them. Then we ride over to Henry's, park our bikes out of sight, and hop the fence. For the first time, we risk climbing the tree in daylight. I jerk my thumb toward the top of the tree: *Up.* Billy wants to go up there and doesn't need my encouragement. We climb, get the plank fitted into place, and there's Henry smiling in his window, ready to go. We help him out. When we're all safe on the ground and back to our bikes, out of ear range of the house, Henry goes goofy with pleasure.

"I'm out, I'm out, I'm out. Out, out, I'm out!"

Georgie is getting his first real look at Henry.

Henry notices this and, quick, turns the corners of his mouth down and puts out his bad hand to show it to Georgie. Georgie is too little to think it is ugly. He likes it and smiles and very gently dabs it once with his fingers, and then, as it doesn't bite him, he pets it. By now Henry is shaking his head and tearing up a little. Billy signs to me, *Enough of that.*

I clap my hands, loud. "Let's go."

I hike Henry on the rack of my bike, and Billy has Georgie, as usual, on his handlebars. On the way to Butter's house Henry starts saying how we still don't want Butter knowing he's our suspect and to leave him be while he, Henry, sniffs things out on his own.

We get to Butter's and knock. "Heeeeelloo, campers!" Butter explodes out his front door in his typical way. I think if Butter weren't always acting like he's running for president or something, trying to impress you, he'd have some friends.

"Who's this?" he says shortly. He whips his eyes up and down Henry, and then it's like two dogs sniffing each other and figuring out right off that they will never get on.

"I'm Henry," says Henry, slipping his claw hand quietly into his pocket.

"Well, good for you," Butter says.

"You have any animals?" Henry says, voice frog-rough, nervous.

"Nope. And it ain't any of your business what I have or don't have."

"Well, you mind if we come in for a drink of water?" Henry says, getting control of himself and trying suddenly to sound cheery as a salesman.

Billy looks at me. We realize Henry isn't smooth about his detecting at all.

"You guys thirsty?" Butter asks.

Georgie says, "I'll have a Coke."

"Really?" Butter looks at Henry again, looks at

me and Billy, and frowns. "Come on, there's a hose in the backyard." We all tramp round there and drink some from the hose, pretending we are thirsty. The water's hot, as it's already past noon and the sun has made the whole sky white with its heat.

"You mind if we go indoors now?" Henry asks.

"Yeah, I do. My mom is trying to sleep, and we have to go to work. I don't know where you come from, but here in the San Joaquin valley, boys havta work."

"Oh . . . sure," Henry says, again with that scaredy-cat, gravelly voice he has for a spare.

"Look, I'm going back in to get a nickel from my mom. Hope you guys have your own if you are planning on a soda today," Butter says. "Or maybe you are planning to buy me one?" He pauses. "No? Didn't think so." He clomps up onto a back porch that's hidden by weeds and opens the back door.

"I have money," Georgie says.

"Yeah, sure you do, kid," Butter says, smiling, and then disappearing into his house.

"Henry, what are you doing?" I whisper hot and loud at him. "You think Butter is stupid or something?"

"I know what I'm doing," he says, voice wavery and low, his eyes looking down at his boots. Billy and Georgie and I all look at his boots too. They're brand-new hiking ones you could cross the Himalayas in if you needed to.

Butter comes slamming right back out, drops down the steps, and comes over to eye Henry directly.

Henry stomps off through the weeds toward Butter's garage. It's got a rusted Masterlock padlock on it. He slides along the side of the garage and shades his eyes, trying to see in the one little window that's there. We all just watch him. He seems as if he's trying to make a show of his detecting.

Butter doesn't seem nervous, just irritated and, maybe, curious. "Where did you get him?" We know what he means 'cause Henry is wearing these safari-like shorts, those expensive hiking boots, a new, pressed shirt, and a yellow bandana knotted round his neck like a cowboy. He's definitely not Orange Grove.

"He's the kid of Mrs. Pineroe's sister's daughter."

"What?"

"More or less her nephew."

"No kidding. Must have money, then, huh?" Butter says with what seems a new appreciation of Henry.

"I have lots of money," Georgie says again. He's itching his belly.

"Georgie, you shouldn't be lying," I say.

"I'm not lying," Georgie says.

"You know the only one has any money is Henry." Georgie isn't impressed.

I don't like being doubted, so I explain. "Henry has his own motorboat, a black stallion—that's a horse—a wireless walkie-talkie, and his own personal bodyguard and servant back home in San Francisco."

"Hey, buddy," Butter calls, teasing, over to Henry, who is still nosing around the garage, "something you're looking for?" Says it nice and Teddy Roosevelt friendly.

Henry looks at Butter like he's been waiting for that. He unties that yellow bandana and mops his face. "No, just looking around at your place." Then he walks over to where we're standing, pulls out a set of keys, and holds them up for everyone to see. Dangles them for us. There's a slim silver whistle hanging with them too.

"This is a dog whistle. My cousin gave it to me a long time ago. I keep it on my key chain."

"Those keys for your motorboat?" asks Georgie.

"What?" Henry says.

Billy and I are eyeing that whistle.

"Can you ski from that boat?" Georgie asks.

Billy reaches out and takes the whistle. Henry lets him.

Billy turns it over in his hand.

"You drive that motorboat in the canal?" Georgie says.

"What's a dog whistle?" I ask, speaking for Billy and myself.

"It's just that. A whistle. Dogs hear it. A whistle for a dog. A dog can't whistle. You whistle a dog. Dog whistle." Henry is getting excited with himself again.

Billy blows into that whistle, but no sound comes.

I shake my head.

He blows again, hard as he can.

"You ever going to bring that boat to our house?"

"Oh, please, Georgie, hush," I snap.

"Maybe you shouldn't have told him all that stuff about me," says Henry, looking my way.

I cut him short. "You have any little brothers?"

"No," Henry says, slow, in the low voice.

Billy's still blowing, his face reddening up and his eyes popping. Still no sound.

"Broken," I say.

"No," Henry says, normal-voiced, "it's perfectly fine. A dog whistle makes a sound so high that humans can't hear it, but a dog will go mad barking when you blow it."

Butter is frowning.

I don't believe Henry, but he insists that it is true. He has Billy keep blowing the whistle and us listening hard between blows, and, sure enough, two doors down, somebody's Chihuahua starts yipping like a coyote pup.

Butter's mom starts hollering for him through the bedroom window at the back of his house. Butter looks genuine worried. I guess having a mom that's so needy might not be much fun. Butter says, "Be right back." He trots across the yard and, just before going inside again, says, "And keep it down!"

Right off Henry says, "I doubt Rufus is anywhere near."

"How are we going to buy him back if we don't know where he is?" Georgie says.

"We aren't trying to buy him yet; we are trying to find him," I say.

"Then what do I do with the money?" Georgie says, rubbing his belly. We all give him a hard look. I squat down and pull up his shirt. He's got an old canvas money belt round his waist.

"Holy moly," I whisper. It has a little zipper that I open, and inside are a number of bills. "Man, oh man" is all I can say.

Billy crouches down too. He signs, *How much?*

"Where did you get this, Georgie?" I say. I'm getting a little confused and stand up and start to shake his shoulders because he isn't telling.

The screen door bangs shut as Butter comes out.

I stop the shaking and say, "Shhh."

"It's seventeen dollars. Uncle Charlie gave it to me to buy Rufus," Georgie says firmly while twisting out of my grasp. "And," he adds in a whisper, "*I get to keep the belt after.*"

Index finger points up and the other hand
slaps it.

Butter doesn't say anything about the money belt
or the dog whistling. In fact, he is not saying anything
about anything. Billy thinks he didn't hear about or
even see the money, and I think if he did, he might be
pretending he didn't. Henry says he was trying to
make Butter nervous on purpose so's he'd make a
mistake and tell on himself some way. I think we just
made Butter mad and suspicious of us.

We do our route, and Butter doesn't help this
time. Says we got all the help we need. Says route
408 doesn't have a paperboy, it has a Mongol horde,
whatever that is.

Henry is no help at all and, in fact, a big bother.
That's 'cause we can't hike him and the papers at the

same time, so we have to walk the whole way, pushing our bikes. Butter peeled off as soon as we were done folding and loading up. He glanced back at us, looking awful careful at Georgie, if you ask me. I know now Butter is a *definite* suspect, even if Rufus ain't at his house.

Henry blows that whistle the whole time we do our route, which only sets all the dogs on every block to barking, but none of them our Rufus. Georgie won't let anyone carry that money but himself. I think he likes the money belt more than the cash, but neither is getting away from him. After we finally finish our route, we go home and collapse around our bikes in the garage.

We know Uncle Charlie would never say anything about our doings. We know nobody at our house has missed Rufus except us—it's only Monday, and Rufus went missing Saturday morning. My sisters never pay him any mind, and my dad and my older brothers are gone most of the time. My mom is always too busy, up to her elbows in dishes and clothes and spaghetti, to think about Rufus at all. But I glance at my watch. "It's time we usually feed Rufus," I say, looking at Billy.

Billy signs, *Don't get Georgie started.*

Georgie watches that signing and understands his name has been used. He swings his head back and forth, studying on our faces. "Rufus could catch rabbits, right, Paolo?"

"Oh, sure."

"I seen him eat grass sometimes."

"Yep. Ate Mrs. Beyer's laundry off her back porch once," I say thinking wistful and admiring of Rufus's specialness.

"Remember the time I let him in—I mean, when he came in that Sunday and ate all the spaghetti right off the table before Grandma and Grandpa got here for dinner?" Georgie says, eyes big and hopeful.

"So that's what happened?" I say.

"It's possible."

I look at Georgie and realize he's struggling to stay an optimist. "Georgie, Rufus can take care of himself till we fetch him home, and that's what we are going to do." I almost convince myself with the telling. I know Rufus don't like missing a meal any more than any other O'Neil.

I tell everybody about Butter's handwriting that I have, how I still need to compare it to the dognapping note that Theresa has. Henry says we should forget that and go straight to concentrating on tracking Butter. Henry uses that shy, gravelly voice and almost a little-girl face when he says it. Billy grabs his shoulders and looks him in the eye until he stops. Georgie takes himself into the corner and starts untying his money belt to look it over some more, and Henry goes over to him, sits down, and helps him. Georgie lets him.

I talk soft to Billy. "What is the reason he is the way he is, you think? What's with the frog voice?"

Billy smirks and signs, *I can't hear him.*

"Oh, yeah. I forget sometimes, Billy."

I see he makes those faces, though.

I realize Henry does make a little-girl face every time, to go along with that scared voice.

It looks like a little-kid face to me. He does it when he's sort of afraid. When he thinks he needs you to like him.

"It don't make me like him."

Same with that hand. Gets you to treat him like Georgie.

"Doesn't work."

Bet it works with somebody. Billy squints, thinking. *Maybe his mom?*

"You think we should slap him some when he does it?" I'm thinking of Sister Alphonsias Ruth Ann, also known to every catechism kid as Attila the Nun. She'll make you stick out your hand and smack it with a ruler if you give her sass and won't quit. I used to sign my name on my papers *Paolo O'Neil, The Greatest in the World,* and she'd make me stay after class and give me a rap on the knuckles, tell me pride was a sin. I didn't see it that way. I just always figured a guy is responsible for keeping his spirits up. I still have my spirit *and* calluses on the knuckles of my right hand.

Billy shakes his head at me.

"I mean for his own good."

Getting slapped ever been good for you?

Billy has me cold there. Then he says something makes me feel like *I've* been slapped silly. Says, *He just needs a little encouragement.*

Take your thumb and show a stamp being licked and placed on the corner of an envelope to show a *letter*.

Then Theresa is standing in the doorway of the garage, same pretty dress on, mascara smudged with three hours of crying over me, I guess. That's understandable, but I know every move I make now is important. I think this really could be the end of me: She's stalked me to my hideout and wants marrying—or genuine boyfriending, at least—'cause she feels she has rights to show up anytime she wants, as I've kissed her and of my own free will. The others sit up and take notice. Everyone staring, all quiet.

"Here," she says, and sticks out an envelope. "I rang the bell and no one answered for a while, so I thought to bring in the mail from your box and this was there. Margarita said you were probably back here." She drops the envelope on the ground and turns and walks off.

I see, quick, it says **Paolo** on the envelope, snatch it up, and go to the doorway. Theresa is to the gate of our yard. "Theresa!" I holler.

She spins around and looks at me, face pale, eyes smeary and ghoulish.

"Come here," I say.

She looks at me, her lower lip trembling.

"Please," I say. I don't feel like being mean to her.

She puts her head down and wipes at her eyes and then starts over to me slowly. She gets in the garage with us, and we are just all there not doing anything but thinking about her until she points at the envelope in my hand. I take a better look. It wasn't mailed, just put in the mailbox, and my name is typed.

Slowly, I open it and take out the letter. Everyone is crowded round to listen while I read it out loud. I read it exactly as it is typed there: "'Bring fifteen dollars to the corner of Palm and Olive. Leave the money in the knothole of Mr. Livingston's tree. Inside the hole will be a note telling you where you can find Rufus later, *if* you leave the money.'"

"Butter is a clever one," Henry says, and then whistles low, shaking his head.

Billy is studying Henry.

Theresa asks, "Why is that?" She's rubbed most of her skin off as well as the mascara and is brick red round the eyes.

"Because this time he types," Henry says, eyes big and excited. "He knew what Paolo was up to asking to see his writing on the receipts. And he doesn't ask for seventeen, he asks for fifteen dollars. He heard Georgie say seventeen, but it throws us off of him, his asking only fifteen."

I nod my head.

Henry continues, his words crowding up like kids in the doorway of a recess line, then spilling out. "And . . . and . . . he . . . he doesn't help on the route today. He goes and makes this note instead and pops it in the mailbox."

"What seventeen dollars?" Theresa asks.

"My seventeen," says Georgie, and holds up his money belt.

"Wha—"

"He got it from Uncle Charlie," I say.

"Seventeen whole dollars?" Theresa says.

"Yep," I say.

"How did you *do* that, Georgie? I would never have thought you guys could—," she says till I cut her off.

"I told him Rufus was stole by somebody bad, and they wanted money," Georgie says.

"And he just gave it to you?"

Georgie nods as if it's the most natural thing in the world and why would she even ask. "I took all that I wanted out of his wallet. Then he told me I should have a safe place for it and got the money belt from inside his dresser. This is my money belt— forever." He gives Theresa a look of warning.

"Theresa," I say, "Uncle Charlie just does stuff like that. When I was Georgie's age, I asked for his gold ring. I didn't understand what I was asking, and he unscrews it off his finger and gives it to me and goes back to playing checkers without blinking. I lost that ring too. Very same day." My voice slips away with remembering.

Let's go, Billy signs.

I look at Theresa.

She raises her eyebrows and shrugs.

"Yes. We drop the money, get the note, and then

keep a watch on that tree, and we'll get him," Henry says.

Everybody looks at one another and nods, except for Georgie, who is strapping his money belt back on and having trouble. Henry helps him, enjoying Georgie's foolishness, I think. Billy is still studying Henry.

Theresa rides on my handlebars, Henry on the back rack, Georgie with Billy on his Schwinn. It's slow going, about the same as pedaling with the Sunday papers. Fortunately, it's only three and a half blocks to Mr. Livingston's tree. I sort of crash-land, slow, into it, Theresa and Henry sort of spilling and hopping off. Billy brings his bike up neatly, and Georgie jumps down.

Georgie won't give up the money till we tell him he can keep the extra two dollars and the money belt. Yes, we tell him, forever and ever and ever; no, not just till we get home and take it back, no. Henry helps him take the money out. It's all in one-dollar bills. Uncle Charlie keeps ones handy to send Hector or Ernie out for Camels.

I lean my bike up against the tree and stand on the seat and hook my arm into the knot of that old oak tree. Scratch around. Nothing. No note.

That's a blow. We discuss it and decide Butter hadn't had time to put a note there yet, but we think we should leave the fifteen dollars anyway. It is Henry who insists, saying that we are going to keep a watch and catch him anyhow. Theresa thinks that if that's the case, we can catch him leaving the note and don't need to leave any money. But Henry seems to have a point when he says maybe Butter has no intention of leaving a note and is just going to come for the money.

"Yes, but—," Theresa starts to say.

"That's it, I am going to go back to my attic and stay there if I have to listen to this girl," Henry says, stomping his feet. He's using his claw to point at Theresa, and she steps away when she sees it and almost stumbles.

"We have to get you home pretty soon anyway, Henry," I say.

Henry scowls. "My aunt brings my dinner up at five o'clock, so she already knows I'm missing."

I check my watch. It's five-thirty. We're missing dinner. Summers, my mom doesn't care, except for Georgie. "Theresa, will you take Georgie home?" I ask.

She wants to stay with us—with me—I can tell. She's miffed at Henry too. Ernie says watch out when a woman looks at you like she's about to dance on your lips in high heels and enjoy it, and that's how Theresa is eyeballing Henry until she finally looks at me and says, "Sure, Paolo." Then, with no sound, she mouths the words, *I'll miss you.* Somehow, she put a little fairy dust on it 'cause, weird as it is, I don't mind her saying it, though I don't answer back. She leaves, taking Georgie.

"Give me the money, Henry." He hands it up to me where I am still standing on my bike. I shove it down into the hole. "Okay, we need to find ourselves a hiding spot. And, Henry, you are going to be in big trouble 'cause we can't take you home till this is over."

He shrugs. "So what's new?"

I notice Billy is studying Henry like he's a bug in science class, and I think, *Oooooh, I get it. He hasn't ruled Henry out as a suspect.*

Your right hand in a C shape placed over your chest where a badge would go means a *cop*.

Henry gets a motorcycle ride from Officer Callahan, who came by on his Harley-Davidson police bike around ten o'clock. Came round that same block where we were in the bushes across the street from Mr. Livingston's tree three times. The fourth time he stops and throws his little searchlight on the bushes and tells us to come out. Tells me and Billy to get home right now. Asks if Henry's name is Henry Demotte, and when Henry says yes, he puts him on the back of the motorcycle, saying, "Okay, chief, hold me around the waist. Hold *tight*." And then he putters off, slow, so as not to scare Henry, I guess, who isn't scared at all, just smiling. Those big twin cylinders sound like *PO-TA-TO, Po-Ta-To, po-ta-to* fading off into the distance.

We get our fifteen dollars back out of the knothole and ride home. Billy has it and insists on holding it for safekeeping. I feel a little like I got kicked in the liver, though. No Rufus and my Timex ticking.

My mom comes down when she hears us come in and warms up some bell peppers stuffed with hamburger and tomatoes. She jabbers in Italian fast as one of those guys at an auction, every once in a while swinging round to point a spatula at me and give me two evil eyes at the same time.

Even though Georgie's been home for some time probably sitting at the table waiting, she grabs him by his ears and kisses the top of his head everytime she passes by him while fussing over our dinner and plates. He's too tired to squirm clear of her, which is good 'cause pinching and kissing and hugging will calm an Italian mother-person better than anything. She gives one of my ears a pinch too, one of those pinches that'll make your ear howl up to your brain like a coyote that's wanting company. She goes up to bed once we're done chewing.

Georgie is dead asleep, and Billy has to move his legs so he can fit in the bed with him. The windows are open, and a night breeze has come up like it does summers once it gets really late. I watch the black silhouettes of the trees throwing their heads about, looking like women bending to shake out their long hair.

Billy thinks I'm asleep and goes to do his usual looking at his notes with his flashlight, except this time he takes out a notebook and writes in it for a few minutes. I've never seen that before and decide that I should remember to check if he's started a story of his own life or what. He writes a little, finishes up, and goes to bed.

I lie there and think about Theresa, and 'cause I'm safe at home in my bed, she doesn't scare me, and I think she is just a nice person, that's all. Nice with soft skin and deep river eyes, lips that are wet peaches, and then I catch myself and make myself stop thinking about her. Instead, I think of Henry and his flipper hand and Billy with his suspicions and Butter and his mom; Georgie, happy with his money belt. Then I remember Rufus, tongue hanging out and tail wagging and always a question in his eyes. I wonder if he's dead then, and I feel like my stomach is an elevator going down into the dark, feel bad as I ever felt in my life.

chapter TWENTY-SEVEN

Put your thumbs to the side of your head, with the other fingers waving like big floppy ears, to show you're a *donkey*.

Next day is a Tuesday, and we do pretty much nothing except our paper route. Butter doesn't talk to us, and we don't bother him. We don't go see Henry, and Billy and I pretty much leave Georgie to himself. He's worried about Rufus, I know, and has taken up an interest in Maria-Teresina-the-Little-Rose again. We got nothing to do and no ideas, so we go over to San Joaquin's to straighten things up behind the altar like Monsignor told us we're supposed to do whenever we have the time. He lets us in and leaves us to mope. That's what grown-ups call staying still, if you are a kid. When *they* do it, they are resting or thinking.

But it is true I am feeling mean-sick about not finding Rufus. I even eat some of the hosts—those paper-thin, quarter-size bits of bread they have for Communion—and wash them down with some wine. That ain't a mortal sin 'cause Monsignor hasn't made them into genuine Communion yet, but I know full well I'm not supposed to be eating somebody's food without being invited, especially the church's.

Doing so is on account I'm mad and I'm worried about Rufus. Hard as I've been trying to think things are just temporary bad the way they mostly always are, I realize this time could be different. Billy just sits there watching me munch, shaking his head, but doesn't sign anything to stop me. He's not sorry for me, either. I think maybe he's ashamed of me. Maybe 'cause of how I'm treating Theresa? I don't really know. Maybe it's 'cause I haven't tried as hard to find Rufus as he thinks I should, though I have. I can't help it if I am "easily distracted." Those are the exact words Sister Alphonsias Ruth Ann wrote with her black ink cartridge pen on my catechism report card a long time ago. Monsignor once said curiosity is a sign of intelligence. He also said that getting excited by your own nosiness is boredom and a sign of stupidity, that I should take care to keep those two inclinations straight.

You know, when you are smarter than most everybody else, it's more a burden than not. Folks think you should be on top of everything all the time. Either that or your smarts scare them and make them feel stupider than they are. Ernie told me one day, believe it or not, that when he was just ten years old, he was sitting in class and suddenly realized he was a racehorse stabled with donkeys. Said from then on he had to pretend he was kin to donkeys and happy about it, too, or else folks would say he was overly fond of himself, which is impossible. Said confidence is what makes a civilization. He said whenever he gets depressed about the whole thing, he reminds himself that even the Lord rode a little donkey—name of Max—whenever there was a parade.

Well, we got through that day without any idea on what to do, and then the next day the newspaper says Theresa's grandma is gone. Or, I should say, it shows it. The only time the *Grove County Guide* runs your picture is if you get arrested or die, so it ain't the usual to see folks you know. We recognize her picture right off like you are supposed to. Still, it's a surprise.

I mean, I knew when I'd seen her that day with Theresa that she was getting close to passing on, but still, it's a shock. It seems your mind knows stuff like that and yet won't let you know it outright, even though it's there plain as day. I remember what Theresa said about getting her grandmother outdoors whenever she could, as it might be her last chance. That's good advice for anyone, I guess. I feel a fist squeeze what might be one of my kidneys when I think of it. It squeezes again when I think how Mrs. Mueller was that old and still interested in knowing if I was Theresa's boyfriend or not.

We have to pay Theresa a call, Billy signs as soon as we put the paper down. We are sitting on the curb out front of our house after doing our route. It's maybe three-thirty. This afternoon is more muggy than hot, kind of gray and gloomy. Like one of those summer storms is going to come over the Sierras and drift down to the valley and is taking its time.

"Billy, that would be butting in on another's trouble."

Billy looks at me. Blinks. Waits a full minute—I

do not know how he can do that, but he can—and blinks again.

"Aw, heck, Billy, you know how Mrs. Bianci hotfoots it over and quizzes Mom every time one of us falls off the roof or whenever Ernie and Hector leave me tied to a tree for the day or when Grandpa has a little wine and plays his saxophone late on a Sunday and gets the neighbors' dogs singing. She always says how she is worried something is wrong and can she help, but she just wants some scrap of gossip to keep the Ladies Altar Society interested in her boring self."

Billy doesn't even blink this time at all. Pushes his lower lip out. Slow.

"Ooooh, well, where are you planning to go? Theresa's house or her grandma's?" I say it like I'm too tired to be much interested one way or another.

We're going to her grandma's first.

"Oh, we are? Why's that?" My voice gets scratchy and gives away that I am troubled. Troubled by Theresa, by Rufus, by my not being able to right things lickety-split like usual. But Billy can't hear how my voice sounds. I don't like it when people get the idea you got feelings about stuff, 'cause they are likely to go and make fun of you. Billy has never done that, but it still is my habit to keep that sort of business to myself.

Billy gets up and starts off down the block. I haven't agreed to anything, but my natural curiosity gets the better of me, and I start after him, trailing maybe forty yards behind. In no time Billy gets out to the road where Mrs. Mueller used to live and then makes his way toward her house, quick, not dawdling or even looking round more than once or twice to see if I'm still with him. We come up on the house, and I see there are no lights on, no curtains open, nothing going on at all. I doubt Theresa is there. No cars are in the driveway, so I know that if she's in there, she's all by herself and sitting in the dark. That would be just like her to want to hang around by her lonesome. But in a place where someone fresh-dead has been? I feel the space between my shinbones and the joints of my knees getting weak. If knees could be dizzy, then that's what they are, so I stop. Watch.

And curious as Billy can be, he is doing what is even more curious than his typical self. He's heading to the front door when he seems to notice something on the ground alongside the house. He cocks his head, bird-like, back and forth, and I'm straining to see what he sees. Then he goes down the drive a bit, crouches on his knees, and I see that he's trying to look in the shuttered little basement windows there just above-ground. Overcast as it is, I can see faint swords of light stabbing out from their edges. Somebody's home.

Now, I ain't frightened, I tell you, just feeling things aren't right, like we are being disrespecting of the dead or like Theresa is going to come out ghost-scared or crying and wanting to hug me forever or something I do not know, and as usual, I can't help myself, can't go against my nature—I take a sharp quick breath, sort of snort, and turn home, trotting, I guess, just as skittish and fast as my racehorse knees will take me.

chapter TWENTY-EIGHT

Make like breaking a stick hard and forever, and naturally, that's a **break**.

Henry gets to go to the funeral 'cause his aunt comes. My mom and my sisters and Georgie and even Hector are there, my dad not, as he is gone on his train. Ernie is up in Tehachapi looking after PG&E's desert pipes and property. Uncle Charlie is there next to my mom, looking pale and confused as to where he is but following my mother's lead with no hint of falling asleep. He reminds me of what an old mule might look like if it were wearing a loose, rumpled suit and were trained to sit upright in a pew.

Theresa's dad and her mom and their whole clan are there. You can tell them by their red hair and their freckles and skin like the thin, sticky stuff that you'd skim off the top of milk you were warming. Theresa's face looks like she hasn't slept in a week, eyes red-rimmed and blank. She's got on a little black dress and a little black cap like those monkeys wear that take pennies from your hand at carnivals.

Her grandma is laid out very pretty in a polished walnut casket that is the nicest piece of furniture any Mueller has probably ever seen. Or me, either. I think it's too bad you can't buy your casket early and use it for a couch or something for a while. But I know it's money spent to show your respect. Theresa's grandma looks as sweet as a body could look with painted roses for cheeks and hair done up blue. I half imagine her sitting up and asking if this is the picnic she's been waiting on.

Funerals are more complicated for altar boys than any other job, as you have to get incense burning and keep it going in a little lantern with holes and hand it to Monsignor at the right times so he can swing it round from a chain in special ways, that smoke perfumed and billowing out, and you can't cough or let on that you're choking. Billy and I do fine, and Monsignor tells how Mrs. Mueller was the friendliest sort and how she was loved, and that's true, you can tell, by all the Muellers sniffling and patting one another on the back and holding hands so they don't faint. I feel one of my kidneys wake up again when I realize I don't want to lose my grandma and grandpa, ever.

After it's over and all are gone, Billy and I straighten everything up, quick. We don't have any duty at the cemetery and are about to leave after snuffing out the candles. The church is a pleasure when no one is around. Quiet and cool and dark and all ours and nothing we have to do.

Billy taps me on the shoulder where I'm standing looking around. I look at him, and he points out to the pews that are all empty except in the back where one little person is sitting alone in the dark. I don't have to think. I know it's Theresa.

I shake my head, *No.* Billy takes my elbow and holds my eyes like he's got a gun on me. I see that Theresa hasn't gone to the graveyard just so's she can talk to me, and that scares me almost to needing burying myself. I figure Billy's visit to Theresa at her grandma's house took care of our family paying their respects. I didn't ask Billy for details on his visit after I left 'cause I figured that would, like as not, end up somehow like this—me having to talk to her.

I know I can probably wait five minutes and her folks will be back in Robinson's Funeral Home's black Lincoln Continental to fetch her, soon as they figure out she's ditched them and stayed here. Billy walks to where the little door behind the altar is, looks at me hard, then disappears.

I still have my altar clothes on and feel some comfort in that—whatever I say will be as part of the job and not personal. I walk slowly down the aisle and stop at her pew. She's not kneeling, but sitting and looking straight ahead.

"Hey," I say.

She gives me a quick look, her eyes hard, so I think I've said the wrong thing, as I have no experience being whatever it is that I am right now.

I try again. "I'm sorry."

Her eyes seem to twist like they are washrags somebody's wringing out.

"About your grandma," I add. I guess I could be sorry about not dropping by and saying anything before today.

"You don't have to pretend you care, Paolo," she says, gone back to looking straight ahead.

"I . . . care," I say.

She quick-peeks at me, eyes shining with pain, like a pigeon I had to stomp and put out of its misery once after it was half chewed up by a cat. She examines me and then looks away.

I just stand there because I don't always know what to do.

"I don't want to see you anymore," she says, talking to the pew in front of her.

"You don't?" I ask, and there is surprise and a little relief in my voice, I think, so I wish I hadn't spoken so quick. I'm also rude lots of times without meaning to be. I think guys do that more than girls, but I'm not sure.

"Just go, Paolo," she says as tight as can be, the way my mom sounds when she's had enough of my foolishness for one day.

And that's it. I am broken up with a girl, by a girl, for the very first time. And you want to know what? It feels a lot like when a pretty teacher in elementary school you'd do anything for, like, say, Mrs. Lewis, is mad at you, mad at you forever 'cause you horsed around one time too many, and she says, sharp and sure, *You are dismissed.*

Motion as if two people are coming face-to-face by pushing the flats of your hands together for just that—*facing someone*.

We leave Georgie home. It's like he's forgotten about Rufus or, like little kids do, is distracted for a while, what with the funeral and his money belt and Maria-Teresina-the-Little-Rose and the like. You can bet, though, just like a little kid, he'll start up pestering the second he remembers. Billy seems more thoughtful than worried about Rufus.

I don't say it, but the funeral has made me start feeling desperate. That very night, long after our route is done and dinner is over, I figure there is no harm and maybe, just maybe, some gain in talking to Henry again. Billy says okay. We go up Henry's tree to talk to him. Henry's mad to go hang out by Mr.

Livingston's knothole again. He doesn't care that his aunt will find out that he's run off again when she comes to tell him good night, 'cause he's getting sent back home in a week anyway, maybe less. What's weird is that once we are all down from the redwood tree outside Henry's attic and getting onto our bikes, Billy signs to me, *Let's go get Butter.*

That's so strange, I tell Henry what he's said.

"Well, we might have a look around Butter's garage again. That might not be a bad idea," Henry says.

I know it's not what Billy meant, but I leave it at that. We pedal into town, looking over our shoulders and listening out the whole time for Officer Callahan's motorcycle. We ride to Butter's house and stash our bikes in what seems a herd of sheep shadows huddled by the bushes next to the house. We creep down the side of the place and go to the window of the garage. Henry blows that dog whistle of his. But Billy isn't even looking at anything except Butter's house. It's got no lights on. Small enough to be a garage itself, broken down and sagging on the west end, moon-bleached with weeds jumped up alongside it.

"Billy," I say, "you satisfied now?"

He's not looking at the lips of what I'm saying and is starting off toward the house.

Henry says, in his frog-nervous voice, "What's he doing?"

Billy is a shadow crossing the yard when suddenly he disappears, as if he's dropped into a hole. I run over, with Henry on my heels, and there is Billy on the ground with Butter holding him in a wrestling scissor-lock hold. Right off I dive atop them both and try to get Butter round the head, but he's thrashing this way and that and I'm having a time of it. Finally, I get one arm round his neck. We are mashing back and forth, all busy with what seems some kind of furious, silent, weird work.

Billy and I are holding our own, but Butter's a large one—a fish one size too big for us. Henry says in his low, shy voice, "Butter, stop that." It sounds so dumb that Butter laughs whilst he's rearranging Billy's legs, twisting them like taffy. Henry says, again, but in his regular voice, "Stop that!"

Billy lets out a little pup yelp of pain, and that must have made Henry forget his fear 'cause he throws himself on top of us, swinging about with his one good arm trying to smack Butter.

Butter is laughing full-out now, and not giving up one bit, when Henry locks his arm round one of Butter's legs and then bites him. Butter howls with surprise and stops fighting sudden and altogether. Billy and I jump clear of him. Henry's still wound onto him with his good arm like a snake's tail and trying to line up for another bite. Butter is scooting round on his hands and butt, and hollering, "Get him off me!" He's in a panic.

Billy grabs Henry around the neck and has to choke him until he starts to go limp or black out to get him to let Butter loose. Then the rear window of Butter's house slams up. His mom hollers, "What is going on? Francis? Francis Bingham, is that you?"

We all go still as thieves.

"Francis, is that you? I am going to call the police this minute if it isn't!"

"It's me!" Butter Francis Bingham Schwartz shouts.

"Well, tell your friends it is high time they went home!"

He calls to her, "Yes, Mother!"

We are all just sitting there. Butter looks crushed, like a sumo wrestler who isn't going to get his dinner. Henry and I are not going to laugh no matter what.

We want to, but if Butter has to go through his life being Francis Bingham, we know that's more than we should laugh at right now.

"You . . . ," I start to say, and Butter shoots me a be-careful-what-you-say look, "should get that bite looked to."

He gets up and walks toward his garage, takes out a key and opens the lock, and goes in. We follow. Suddenly, there is light, Butter standing there with a string in his fist that runs up to a bare bulb. Butter sits down on a steel locker and pulls up his pant leg. There's a little purple half-moon of a bite mark but no blood.

He looks at Henry and shakes his head. "I ought to kill you."

Henry looks at him, raising his eyebrows, and I look at Butter, smiling. And right there a deal is struck without any talking at all. Henry gets to live, and Butter, well, that's the only name he'll ever have to answer to round Orange Grove.

Your hand makes like it's on someone's head and moves upward, showing you're measuring them *growing up*.

Billy puts out his hand for Henry to shake, and Henry puts out his good hand, which is his left. Billy shakes his head and nods toward the right, the little flipper. Henry raises it, and Billy grabs it and shakes it. Henry smiles and says, "Thanks." Says it in his regular-boy voice with his regular-boy face. And at that Billy nods with approval. They stand there a minute, hands locked, eyes locked, and some agreement I'm not sure of takes place.

It occurs to me for the first time that Billy gets his own encouragement by giving it to other kids.

Finally, Butter grunts. "What are you guys doing over here this time of night, anyway?"

I look at Billy.

He lets go of Henry and signs to me, kind of shy, *I thought, from now on, Butter might like to be in on whatever we do. That's all.* He smiles the kind of smile where your mouth is a flat line. *And he doesn't have Rufus, if you haven't figured that out yet.*

Now, that's more than Billy says in a week, so I put some thought on it.

"What's he say?" Butter asks. "I can't ever figure out that . . . dog talk of his."

I know Butter hasn't meant to be rude, so I let him off the hook. "Says you can hang out with us whenever you want. And it is sort of like dog talk. You pay attention to the signs, and a dog will tell you as much as a person."

"No kidding," he says. "Hang out with you whenever I want? What makes you think I want to do that?" He tries to act like he couldn't care less, which isn't the case.

"So don't if you don't want to," I say.

Billy smirks and looks around and up at the bare lightbulb of that garage.

Henry says, "You don't have Rufus?"

"You could have just asked me that a long time ago, ya know," Butter says, looking Henry in the eye. "No,

I don't have him, and I never have. What about *you*?"

Henry blushes and sputters, "Me?" But for the first time when he's unsure of himself, he hasn't used that nervous-shamed voice.

"Butter," I say, "will you help us look for him?"

"Sure," he says, "and I might have a pretty good idea where we should look."

Your forefinger is upright and moves straight forward out from your mouth to show you speak the ***truth***.

But Butter doesn't have a chance to tell us. Instead, his mom comes out in her flannel nightgown, shaking like it's cold, which it isn't, and wobbly on her feet but hollering plenty loud, "You boys get home this instant!" So we take off right quick, leaving Butter to his mom, who is rattling on at him with worry. He's calm and acting more like the parent than she is, leading her back inside their little house. We get Henry home and up the tree, across the plank, and into his room. Soon as he is inside, the light goes on, and we hear his aunt screeching at him. We scoot down the tree almost as fast as firemen on one of their poles since we've done it many times now.

We get our bikes and ride home, the whole sky to ourselves and so huge it makes me think of Mr. Gladstone's giant newspaper machine stamping out its thousands and thousands of black letters—except this time they are white stars spilled everywhere.

Since we've just seen Henry's aunt and Butter's mom do like they were trying out for the movies as witches who've been on diets too long, we are glad when we get home and no one is there who wants to get after us. Georgie is asleep. Billy climbs in with him and in no time starts a little soft snoring.

But I can't sleep and slip out of bed, find Billy's flashlight, snatch his notebook, and get back into my bed. I know that it's wrong to read someone's thoughts that weren't meant for you, but sometimes I can't help doing stuff like that. I pull the covers over my head and start reading. The first thing I notice is that there are no dates for any of the stuff Billy has written. Just little scraps he must have jotted down when he felt like it.

Night is your mother's hand. It covers your eyes. You are swimming. Your voice is a bell coming over the water and everyone wants to hear it.

Is Henry's hand a curse on him
only because he can't forget it?
Maybe I'm like him, never forget
that I can't talk and what do people think
about that.

Paolo has the devil in him.
Not the real devil, just a horse
too big for him or something,
a bucking horse he tries to ride.
Boy-on-a-Bucking-Horse
is one of his names in my head this week.
The other name is Best-Friend-for-Life.

I'm reading fast now, hungry to see what someone
thinks when they think no one can know it.

Maybe Mr. Gladstone wants to be my dad.
I already have one. I don't know him, but
he is my dad and I can't have another.
I mean, Mr. Gladstone could be a secret
dad that I talk to when I want to.
Who would ever think I would have a dad
that was bald and yelled at everybody
except me and Mr. Weinchek?

Theresa takes good care of Rufus. I saw
through the little window in the ground
into her grandma's basement. I never will
shame her for stealing him just to get Paolo,
who is possibly in love with her,
to pay her attention. She must be
even more lonely now her grandma is gone.
If I tell on her no one will ever be her friend.
I can just let Rufus loose myself soon as
the funeral is over. She will probably let
him loose herself. The only thing is Rufus
looks bored.

The only thing is this family
eats spaghetti mostly. I would like
to have some cheeseburgers,
a bologna sandwich on white bread,
fried chicken with gravy biscuits.

I wonder who it is I am writing to
in this notebook.

Does Spiderman keep notes?

Butter saw that I fold the papers
faster than anybody. Butter has eyes
to see which is more than I can say
for most. What is the use
of talking the way everybody
but me can do if you never notice
what is good in a person and say that?

This is something I can never say.
I touched Theresa's grandmother's hand
when she was in the box. Her fingers
were like cold candles that will never
burn anymore. For a minute I wanted
to get inside with her and close the lid
and see if I would care to go in the ground
for good. I did not. Having no dad and no
voice is not like being lonely forever
in a wood box built exactly for yourself.

Paolo what if you are reading this
and I am sneaking up on you
and going to choke you right now?

chapter THIRTY-TWO

Forefinger touches forehead and then wiggles away, showing that your thoughts are things that slip away like *dreams*.

You ever wake up and can't move? And try, hard as you will, you can't even lift one finger? You think maybe you are dreaming, but you know you aren't; then you wake up and you can move because you were dreaming after all. That happened to me, and for a minute I was wishing it weren't a dream. Wishing I were paralyzed so that I would never have to talk to anybody again. And they could just come and feed me with tubes and talk to me if they thought I could hear them and not if they didn't.

I know I've overslept 'cause the bedroom is empty and the sun is coming in like light flashing off of sheet metal. I feel like if I don't move right this instant, I won't be here anymore, like I will just stop completely, this instant, being real. But I go on lying here anyway, and I don't disappear.

And then I hear a dog barking, going crazy with barking, and slowly I realize it isn't one dog, it's a whole lot of them. So I am able to go to the window and look down in our yard. Most of my family is down there.

Rufus is there, and he's barking and tearing around and then coming back to lick Georgie's face. And my grandpa Leonardo is there, turning in circles trying to keep track of them. And my mom and my sisters are there too. Even Ernie is there because it's Saturday and he's off, and he's holding hands with a dark-headed girl wearing plum-colored lipstick.

And there are six, maybe eight dogs running round our yard, and there is Mr. Hartoonian looking like a giant bowling pin in brown slacks and a yellow Hawaiian shirt. A good-looking guy with a beard is standing next to him, with Margarita and Shawna there looking up at him, him kind of laughing and pretending he isn't getting all the attention they're giving him.

I watch this from my upstairs window, and it is a

picture that is rushing up to me, rushing up to my brain that I know will make sense of it when it gets there. I remember once when I was little driving with Ernie out in the country at night back toward town, and it was like we were sitting still and the city lights were rushing toward us, and it is like that now. And then everything arrives, and I know that man is Mike and those are his sled dogs. And that is Rufus knowing this is his yard and those dogs his special guests. And there is Billy.

Well, I shoot down there as fast as I can. Or I try. I about kill myself when I come to Maria-Teresina-the-Little-Rose, who is, it turns out, climbing the stairs to get me. "You have to wear your clothes in the day," she says after I sit her up where she'd stumbled. I race back upstairs and get dressed and come back down, scooping her up and putting her, piggyback-style, on my shoulders. I come outside, and there is so much commotion that no one notices me in particular, except Billy and then Grandpa, who takes Maria-Teresina-the-Little-Rose for his own shoulders.

Those dogs are loping about back and forth, running our back lot, then over to Mike or Rufus and then off again. They run floating on deer legs, chests tilting up, but then, as their front paws come down, they grab the earth and pull hard at it, slingshotting themselves forward, tongues flinging out and alongside their happy wolf heads. Billy tells me Mr. Hartoonian has picked them all up from the train last night and is showing them off all over town today, driving them round in his truck. Margarita has just asked everybody to dinner whilst looking only at Mike, and my mom has chimed in, of course, with "Yes, yous do come" and so on.

I go over to Georgie. He is tired out from chasing Rufus and getting chased. "Hi, Georgie," I say.

"You can't have my seventeen dollars," he says.

"Good morning to you too" is all I answer.

Billy taps me on the shoulder. Obviously, he's already given Georgie the money back. Now he's nodding toward Ernie and his Italian beauty. Points at his ring finger and nods back toward the girl. I see she's sporting a ring of the engagement kind. Ernie is talking to my grandpa now, and Grandpa is inspecting the girl while pretending to inquire about the weather in the desert this past week. Her quick black eyes and black hair match Ernie's perfect, and I see she is a lovely one, a Mother Mary, and that

Ernie must have that fairy dust sticky all over himself like pollen on a honeybee's legs.

He can hardly speak and just watches her talking to Grandpa, with her eyelashes like big monarch butterflies batting slowly. And she laughs easy, and she touches Grandpa's elbow, and her laughing sounds like a stream bubbling over smooth rock, and it's clear it's pleasing to Grandpa.

Then Rufus comes barreling for me, plows smack into me, and I fall down, and he licks my face like he'd do when I was Georgie's age. I don't even care, I'm laughing so much.

chapter THIRTY-THREE

Forefinger touches forehead showing
thinking.

Everybody does come over to dinner, but I stay up in my room. I think I'll have to watch out or I'll end up like Uncle Charlie. But it's just that I am putting some thought on things, and you have to do that alone. Henry is going back to his mother tomorrow, and Billy and I went to say good-bye today and invited Mrs. Pineroe to trust him with us next summer. We just went to the front door.

"Mrs. Pineroe, we are here to say good-bye to Henry," I said when she opened the door, looking foul at us, Billy and me. But she went and got him, taking an ice age but getting him.

He bounced down the stairs, shouted, "Hi, fellas!"

"Hi," I said, but Billy really lit up and waved hello,

and Henry came over and shook hands with him, using the flipper hand again, this time without hesitating one bit. Mrs. Pineroe noticed that in particular, and she did some kind of calculation in her head, then asked us in for tea or a Coke. We took the Coke, and while she was getting it, Henry wanted to know what we were going to do next about Rufus. I told him Rufus showed up out of the blue this morning and I guess we'd never know who stole him, and before Henry could ask any more, Billy started making signs about next summer, asking if Henry would be coming, and so I started explaining that.

Henry told us he wouldn't do any running away this winter, so come next summer, he could be let out to roam with us. Said he'd bring his bicycle next time. When we left, Mrs. Pineroe had us stand on the porch, all with our arms on each other's shoulders, while she tried to take our picture with a box camera. She was so shaky, I don't think it will come out, but it doesn't matter 'cause we have it in our heads.

Now I am just lying on my bed thinking of Butter, how he'll probably hang with us most all the time, I'll bet, or at least as long as we have our paper route. In fact, today when all was going on at our house, he came by to remind us that we still had our route and don't forget it. We have to be up at five a.m. Sunday, tomorrow, like it or not. I like it about as much as I don't. I'm still waiting till we get to collect money from folks, but that won't happen till the end of the month. Some of my customers know my name and wave when they see me, which Butter says is good and might mean tips, says always wave back in spite of your mood, which I already know.

I think about Theresa and wonder at what she did. How it was her all along. Just a person wanting company too much, which is the same reason for almost everything every person does, good or bad, if you really think about it. I see how every time I told her to get lost, I'd end up needing her to find Rufus. I guess on account she had him safe all the time, she didn't think what she was doing was that bad. She doesn't seem that scary to me since she broke up with me, but she is still mostly a mystery. I guess you can't figure everything out nice and easy.

'Cause of Billy, nobody knows she did it. I don't let on to Billy that I know. Telling the truth to every-body in this case wouldn't do one good thing for anybody, and what the heck is wrong with a secret once in a while; is the whole earth going to stop turning or something?

I hear everyone downstairs, hear all the dishes and the glasses pinging and hear Mr. Hartoonian's big booming laugh. Hear Ernie hushing everyone so he can start in on a story. Probably half of what's being said down there isn't true—and so what? But I wonder what part of Theresa kissing me was true. And what about the part when I was kissing her back? So I know there is more that I have to know.

chapter THIRTY-FOUR

Your middle finger moves out and downward from your mouth, and that's *luck*.

"Georgie, will you quit fooling with Rufus and just come the heck on if you're coming?" It's Sunday, five-thirty a.m., and past time for us to go. Billy wants to get going too.

"Why is it he can't come with us?" Georgie asks.

"Because we just got him back. You wouldn't want him to run off again, would you, Georgie?"

"Going to work isn't running off."

"What do you know about work?"

"I've had lots of jobs," Georgie says, adjusting Rufus's collar and looking back over his shoulder at me where I am all saddled up, ready to go.

"Like what, exactly?"

"I been a paperboy and a detective and a doughnut-eater and a money-carrier . . ."

I close my eyes and shake my head. "Bring the dog."

"Not a dog. It's Rufus."

I open my eyes and see Billy is smiling.

It's mostly dark, and as we are riding, I see that it must have rained a little last night. The black streets are shiny and slick, and even the wind is up this little bit and sharp for summer. But when we get there, inside the paperboy hut, it's warm and light, and all the guys are scurrying everywhere getting their gear, horsing round, hollering, and teasing one another. We go in, Rufus, too, who walks in a little wary until he sees everyone is too busy to mind him, so he does a kind of quick sashaying in, like a baby elephant, along with us as we get our papers, get them folded and bagged, and then loaded onto my bike. Mr. Henderson comes out as we are about to shove off and asks how things are going. "Things are going good," Georgie says. "I've made seventeen dollars."

Mr. Henderson cocks his head. Georgie lifts his shirt and shows him the money belt, then puts his fingers to his lips. "Shhh."

Mr. Henderson opens his mouth to speak but doesn't, knows that it's better not to ask too much about his boys, as Butter says, unless he gets complaints from customers or they don't fork over all they owe the *Guide* come the end of the month. I wave and we move off. Mr. Henderson turns around, goes slowly back into that little place where he's spending his life.

We do our route pretty fast. Billy, carrying one bag on the handlebars of his bike, takes care of one whole block himself whilst Georgie and me do the others. Georgie trots along, and Rufus ranges up and down the block nosing in on gopher and cat smells wherever he can get them.

Butter swings by as we are finishing up. Has his white bag of doughnuts with a grease spot at the bottom, says Mr. Weinchek made sure to put ones in for us, invites us to his house for radio and news-paper comics. Billy signs, *Yes,* and for once I let him go alone, let him have a friend all to himself—I say I'm going home. Billy looks at me funny for a second and then smiles. Butter wants Georgie to come along too. But when Georgie understands they will give him his doughnut and mine whether he goes with them or not, he decides he'd just as soon come home with me, and so we set off.

Georgie, who's on the back rack of my bike now, sounds as if he's munching both doughnuts when he asks, "Paolo, who was it had Rufus all this time?"

I knew that'd be coming. "Nobody," I say. "He was just gone wandering for a while."

"Like Mike to Alaska?"

"Sort of, except Mike's going back."

"You think seventeen dollars is enough to get me to Alaska?"

"Sure, if you don't mind going parcel post."

"What's that?"

"Well, it's going more cramped than you'd like."

"How's that?"

"Well, imagine that you lived in a house smaller than one of the drawers where you put your undershorts."

"I'm imagining."

"And that house is getting thrown round in train cars and bus stations, and just suppose it lands upside down for a couple of days and you with no way out. That's pretty tough living, Georgie."

"Yeah," he says. "Paolo, have you traveled lots of places?"

"No. Been to the same places more than once, though."

I look back at him on the rack of my bike, where he's bumping along watching Rufus, one hand clutching the rack and one holding the second doughnut he's eating; he's not really all that interested in my talk.

Just then we are coming by Theresa's house. It's a little gingerbread castle with a tiny round tower for the place where you go in the front door. I stop pedaling and glide by slow, and I see Theresa just happens to be sitting on her front steps alone at seven-thirty in the morning like I thought she might be. I stop the bike. "Georgie, you mind staying here with the bike for a second?" I ask.

"Nope," he says, and yawns a mash of doughnuts.

"And can you keep an eye on Rufus?"

"'Course I can," he says, swallowing hard.

"All right, then. You stay here," I say, swallowing hard myself. I get off the bike and snap the kickstand down. It's the heavy-duty kind and can hold Georgie sitting on the rack, where he stays. I go up to the porch. Theresa stands up, fright in her eyes, like maybe she's about to run inside.

"Hey, Theresa," I say, before she can decide.

"Hey, Paolo," she says, weak, and turns back to me, but with her eyes to the ground. I don't know how, but she knows that I know about Rufus. Maybe Billy had to talk to her to get him out of that basement. Anyway, she figures I know, I can see that.

"How are you doing?" I say, coming up one step.

"I'm okay." She looks off across the street where the morning sun is painting the houses yellow and pink. "Just miss her, that's all," she says, soft. She means her grandma. She looks up to catch a quick peek at my eyes, sees I'm not there to accuse her.

"Yeah," I say. Though I don't know what that means, exactly.

"Yeah," she says. Sounds smarter coming from her.

"You'll be spending most of your time round here, then, huh?" I motion with my head to her house.

"Yes."

"That's what I figured." She drops her head again, her eyes wet with shame or sorrow or both, and I think my stopping was curiosity and kindness, but it's not helping.

"I'm sorry," she says so quiet, I almost think I've imagined it. Her red hair, hanging low with her head, lifts suddenly with a gust of wind, and she brings her hand up to catch that hair blowing away from her face, and that's a photograph I'll have with me always.

"Me too." And I mean it. Then it's quiet. "Well, I'll see you around," I say. No kissing. No wanting to kiss. No being scared of it, either, though I know I will see her around my whole life that I live in Orange Grove. I see my life is a mystery that will always be of interest, wanting to see how it will turn out. And I walk back, slow, to Georgie.

Rufus is gnawing the rear tire, and I pull him away without thinking. I mount up and we move off. Georgie is awful quiet, but I know he hasn't fallen asleep on account he was probably paying close attention to Theresa and me.

"Say, what are your plans for that seventeen dollars?" I holler back to him, loud, for some reason.

"I don't have seventeen dollars, Paolo."

"Maybe you'd like to invest in this paper route of mine."

"I don't have any dollars." We are moving along now at a fast, rocky clip.

"Say that you give me the seventeen, and when I collect from my customers, you get some of a percent for the rest of your life or until you are seven years old, whichever comes first."

"Okay," Georgie says, his voice bouncy as the bike 'cause we are flying along. "Could you take an IOU?" he hollers back.

I'm surprised he knows what that is and say, still shouting, "I'll take the seventeen in cash, Georgie."

"I gave it to Mr. Harimoto," he says, not yelling, but I hear him and hit the brakes hard, laying down a three-foot black rubber skid on the sidewalk. Flick the kickstand down, hop off, yank Georgie's shirt up, and unzip the money belt. He has his hands up as if he's being robbed and doesn't care. It's stuffed with Billy's newspaper clippings about Mickey Mantle. "Georgie, what did you do that for?"

"For one of those little trees."

"What?"

"One of those bonze . . . eyes. For Uncle Charlie."

I sigh, near to weeping, about the money, not Theresa, I tell myself.

"On account he never hardly gets outdoors."

"Right."

"Say, you going to marry Theresa?"

"Not this week, Georgie."

Since we have stopped, Rufus is standing with his head on Georgie's lap; Georgie is pulling his ears out to the sides like airplane wings, gentle-like, with Rufus happy to have him do it. They're awful glad to be back together, you can tell.

"That's lucky," Georgie says, looking up from Rufus at me, looking at my eyes.

"You think so, do you?" Theresa's perfume is still lingering round in my head.

"Yep, because Ernie says it costs lots to marry."

I smile at him, and it's slow, but it's a real one and big, spreading out over my whole face. I swing my leg over the bike, stand up on the pedals, bear down hard, and we begin to move. "Aw, shoot, Georgie," I say. "You know we don't need luck—we work."

One hand slides down the side of the other hand and then slips straight down, sudden, as if off a cliff, which shows this is **The End**.